你一定要學會「看圖英作文」

　　在市政府或學校舉行的英語演講比賽中，指定題目可以事先準備，只要背就行了；但是「看圖即席演講」，題目當場公布，準備時間只有五分鐘。很多參加演講比賽的同學，成敗的關鍵都在「看圖即席演講」。「看一張圖片敘述」的題型，在新的「TOEIC 口說測驗」、「中級複試測驗」和「中高級複試測驗」中，都是固定的題型，同學學會「看圖英作文」，可以一舉數得。

　　「大學入學學科能力測驗」，98 年出現過一次「看一張圖片英作文」，有兩萬多個同學零分，表示很多人都放棄，其實只要用「一口氣英語」的方式，以三句為一組，四組 12 句，大約就可以達到 120 字左右；再以「人事時地物」為出發點，說明過去發生了什麼事，現在情況如何，未來可能發生的情形，再說明你的看法即可。

　　每篇範文我們都附有一個標題，同學考試時，寫或不寫都可以。每個人看到圖片所產生的解讀也許會不同，但只要合情合理，並能符合圖片所傳達出的訊息，並不一定要和範文的情節內容一致。

　　本書之所以能順利地完成，是一個團隊的力量，內容由美籍老師 Laura E. Stewart 編寫，白雪嬌小姐負責設計封面，劉宜芳小姐負責編輯，謝靜芳老師協助校閱，黃淑貞小姐負責設計版面，非常感謝他們的付出。雖然編校製作過程嚴謹，但恐仍有疏失之處，尚祈各界先進不吝指正。

劉毅

如何寫「看圖英作文」

1. 把自己當作一個電視記者，報導圖片中的情況。
2. 看到圖片後，儘量寫出圖片中發生事情的時間和地點，要具有想像力，自行編造。
3. 寫出主要人物是誰。
4. 寫出他在做什麼。
5. 如果有次要人物，就要寫出次要人物在做什麼。
6. 如果有招牌或標語，就可利用上面的英文字來造句。
7. 可寫出圖片中之前的情況。
8. 可寫出圖片中現在的情況。
9. 可寫出未來可能發生的事。
10. 可寫出自己的感覺。

【例】

　　看到人物，就給他取個名字，再來判斷時間及地點，帶出所要描述的主題與事件。

　　Jim's birthday was ***in the summer***.（吉姆的生日在夏天。）
　　【點名主要人物吉姆，將主題定爲吉姆的生日，並由圖片
　　　中人物穿著無袖上衣，可判斷出季節爲夏季】

He decided to ***hold the party in a park***.

（他決定在公園裡辦派對。）

【辦派對為主要事件，並將事件所發生的地點描述出來】

He will ***have a barbecue to celebrate his birthday***.

（他將會辦一個烤肉會慶祝他的生日。）

【為了生日所辦的烤肉會，把主題與事件連結起來】

　　你至少要會寫兩個男生和兩個女生的名字，名字不要拼錯。你看到圖中男生出現了，你就可以給他取名叫 Jim（吉姆）或 John（約翰）等；如果是女生，你就給她取名為 Jennifer（珍妮佛）或 Angela（安琪拉）等。

　　將人、事、時、地、物各項點明出來後，再推測未來可能發生的情形。看到這張圖片，可以馬上寫出三句：

All of Jim's friends will come to the party.

（吉姆所有的朋友都會來參加派對。）

Someone will bring a big birthday cake, and others will bring salad and fruit.

（有人會帶個大生日蛋糕來，而其他人會帶沙拉和水果。）

Some people will give Jim beautifully wrapped gifts.

（有些人會送吉姆包裝得很漂亮的禮物。）

注意事項

1. 字體一定要工整，最好用印刷體。寫出你背過的東西，比較有信心，不會錯。

2. 可適當使用標點符號，愈多不同的標點符號，顯得文章很生動。

3. 第一段說明過去發生了什麼事，而產生目前的情況，故時態通常用過去式；第二段依照目前的情況，推測未來會發生的事，故時態多用未來式。

4. 發揮想像力，依據圖片，描述出合理的人、事、時、地、物。儘量用你曾經學過的句子，寫起來就有信心，字體就會工整。

5. 英文作文「起承轉合」的用法，也可用在「看圖英作文」中，按照起、承、轉、合，背一些轉承語：

(1) 有關「起」的轉承語：

① at present（現在），這個轉承語很好，present 通常當形容詞，是指「現在的」，當名詞是「禮物」。「介系詞＋形容詞」形成的成語不多，能夠寫會讓人家佩服。

② it goes without saying that…（不用說…）這個轉承語很多文章都可以用。

③ generally speaking（一般說來）

④ to begin with（首先）

⑤ first of all（首先）

⑥ It's often said that…（常常有人說…）

⑦ recently（最近）

(2) 有關「承」的轉承語：

① after a few days（幾天之後）

② for example（例如）

③ after a while（過了一會兒）

④ consequently（因此；結果），你寫作文會寫這個字，不拼錯，就有加分的作用。

⑤ in other words（換句話說）

⑥ in particular（特別地），這個成語由「介系詞＋形容詞」形成。

⑦ everybody knows that（每個人都知道）

(3) 有關「轉」的轉承語：

① at the same time（同時）　② in the same way（同樣地）

③ fortunately（幸運地）　④ unfortunately（不幸地）

⑤ on the contrary（相反地）

⑥ on the other hand（另一方面）

⑦ but it's a pity that⋯（但是很可惜⋯）

(4) 有關「合」的轉承語：

① in conclusion（總之）　② in brief（簡言之）

③ as a consequence（因此）　④ as a result（結果）

⑤ to sum up（總之）　⑥ above all（最重要的是）

⑦ eventually（最後）

範例

Jim's birthday was in the summer. He wanted to have a party with his friends. *But* Jim has a lot of friends, and his house is small. *Therefore*, he had to find a bigger place. *Finally*, he decided to hold the party in a park. He will have a barbecue to celebrate his birthday.

All of Jim's friends, around fifty people, will come to the party. He will cook a lot of hamburgers, hot dogs, and chicken for them. Someone will bring a big birthday cake, and others will bring salad and fruit. After the feast, they will sing songs and tell stories and jokes. Some people will give Jim beautifully wrapped gifts. He will never forget this special party.

CONTENTS

TEST 1

提 示

請根據下方圖片的場景，描述整個事件發生的前因
後果。文章請分兩段，第一段說明之前發生了什麼
事情，並根據圖片內容描述現在的狀況；第二段請
合理說明接下來可能會發生什麼事，或者未來該做
些什麼。文長約 120 個單詞（words）左右。

The Barbecue Party

Jim's birthday was in the summer. He wanted to have a party with his friends. *But* Jim has a lot of friends, and his house is small. *Therefore*, he had to find a bigger place. *Finally*, he decided to hold the party in a park. He will have a barbecue to celebrate his birthday.

All of Jim's friends, around fifty people, will come to the party. He will cook a lot of hamburgers, hot dogs, and chicken for them. Someone will bring a big birthday cake, and others will bring salad and fruit. *After the feast*, they will sing songs and tell stories and jokes. Some people will give Jim beautifully wrapped gifts. He will never forget this special party.

1. The Barbecue Party

1. 烤肉會

Jim's birthday was in the summer.

吉姆的生日在夏天。

He wanted to have a party with his friends.

他想跟他的朋友們舉辦派對。

But Jim has a lot of friends, and his house is small.

但是吉姆有很多朋友,而且他的家很小。

Therefore, he had to find a bigger place.

因此,他必須找個更大的地方。

Finally, he decided to hold the party in a park.

最後,他決定在公園裡辦派對。

He will have a barbecue to celebrate his birthday.

他將會辦一個烤肉會慶祝自己的生日。

**

barbecue (ˈbɑrbɪ,kju) *n.* 烤肉
party (ˈpɑrtɪ) *n.* 派對　　***have a party*** 舉辦派對
therefore (ˈðɛr,for) *adv.* 因此
finally (ˈfaɪn̩lɪ) *adv.* 最後　　decide (dɪˈsaɪd) *v.* 決定
hold (hold) *v.* 舉辦　　celebrate (ˈsɛlə,bret) *v.* 慶祝

All of Jim's friends, around fifty people, will come to the party.

吉姆所有的朋友，大約五十個人，都會來參加派對。

He will cook a lot of hamburgers, hot dogs, and chicken for them.

他將為他們準備很多的漢堡、熱狗，和雞肉。

Someone will bring a big birthday cake, and others will bring salad and fruit.

有人會帶一個大生日蛋糕來，而其他人會帶沙拉和水果。

After the feast, they will sing songs and tell stories and jokes.

在盛宴結束後，他們會唱歌並說故事及笑話。

Some people will give Jim beautifully wrapped gifts.

有些人會送吉姆包裝得很漂亮的禮物。

He will never forget this special party.

他將永遠不會忘記這個特別的派對。

** ————————————————

around〔ə'raʊnd〕*adv.* 大約

hamburger〔'hæmbɝgɚ〕*n.* 漢堡

hot dog 熱狗   chicken〔'tʃɪkɪn〕*n.* 雞肉

salad〔'sæləd〕*n.* 沙拉   fruit〔frut〕*n.* 水果

feast〔fist〕*n.* 盛宴   joke〔dʒok〕*n.* 笑話

beautifully〔'bjutəfəlɪ〕*adv.* 漂亮地

wrap〔ræp〕*v.* 包   gift〔gɪft〕*n.* 禮物

TEST 2

提示

請根據下方圖片的場景，描述整個事件發生的前因
後果。文章請分兩段，第一段說明之前發生了什麼
事情，並根據圖片內容描述現在的狀況；第二段請
合理說明接下來可能會發生什麼事，或者未來該做
些什麼。文長約 120 個單詞（words）左右。

An Amazing Discovery

A new city building was going up in Centerville. The workers were digging in the ground to lay the foundation. One of them found something very strange. It was an ancient artifact. The museum sent some archaeologists to investigate. They set up a fence around the site and began to dig.

The scientists will dig systematically so that they do not miss any important artifacts. They will find many interesting things such as pots and weapons. They will discover that it is a buried city. The government will decide to put its building somewhere else so that the excavation can continue. *Eventually*, the whole ancient city will be unearthed. *Then* the city will build a museum so that everyone can learn about it.

2. An Amazing Discovery　　2. 驚人的發現

A new city building was going up in Centerville.

中央村正在蓋一棟全新的城市建築。

The workers were digging in the ground to lay the foundation.

工人們正在挖地基。

One of them found something very strange.

其中一位發現某個很奇怪的東西。

It was an ancient artifact.

那是個古代的文物。

The museum sent some archaeologists to investigate.

博物館派了一些考古學家來調查。

They set up a fence around the site and began to dig.

他們在那個地點的周圍設置柵欄，並開始挖掘。

**────────────

amazing〔ə'mezɪŋ〕*adj.* 驚人的　　discovery〔dɪ'skʌvərɪ〕*n.* 發現
go up 蓋起　　worker〔'wɜkɚ〕*n.* 工人
dig〔dɪg〕*v.* 挖　　ground〔graʊnd〕*n.* 地面
lay〔le〕*v.* 奠定　　foundation〔faʊn'deʃən〕*n.* 基礎；地基的
ancient〔'enʃənt〕*adj.* 古代的　　artifact〔'artɪ,fækt〕*n.* 文物
museum〔mju'ziəm〕*n.* 博物館
archaeologist〔,arkɪ'alədʒɪst〕*n.* 考古學家
investigate〔ɪn'vɛstə,get〕*v.* 調查　　***set up*** 設置
fence〔fɛns〕*n.* 圍牆；柵欄　　site〔saɪt〕*n.* 地點

The scientists will dig systematically so that they do not miss any important artifacts.

科學家們將會有系統地挖掘，這樣他們才不會遺漏任何重要的文物。

They will find many interesting things such as pots and weapons.

他們會發現許多有趣的東西，像是茶壺和武器。

They will discover that it is a buried city.

他們會發現這是一個埋於地下的城市。

The government will decide to put its building somewhere else so that the excavation can continue.

政府將決定把建築物置於別處，這樣挖掘工作才能繼續。

Eventually, the whole ancient city will be unearthed.

最後，整個古城將會被挖掘出來。

Then the city will build a museum so that everyone can learn about it.

接著，該市會建立一座博物館，如此一來大家都可以了解它。

** ————————————————

scientist〔'saɪəntɪst〕*n.* 科學家
systematically〔ˌsɪstə'mætɪkl̩ɪ〕*adv.* 有系統地
so that 如此一來；以便於   interesting〔'ɪntrɪstɪŋ〕*adj.* 有趣的
pot〔pɑt〕*n.* 茶壺   weapon〔'wɛpən〕*n.* 武器
discover〔dɪ'skʌvɚ〕*v.* 發現   buried〔'bɛrɪd〕*adj.* 埋葬的
government〔'gʌvɚnmənt〕*n.* 政府   ***somewhere else*** 在別處
excavation〔ˌɛkskə'veʃən〕*n.* 挖掘   continue〔kən'tɪnju〕*v.* 繼續
eventually〔ɪ'vɛntʃʊəlɪ〕*adv.* 最後   whole〔hol〕*adj.*，整個的
unearth〔ʌn'ɝθ〕*v.* 挖掘   learn〔lɝn〕*v.* 了解

TEST 3

提 示

請根據下方圖片的場景，描述整個事件發生的前因
後果。文章請分兩段，第一段說明之前發生了什麼
事情，並根據圖片內容描述現在的狀況；第二段請
合理說明接下來可能會發生什麼事，或者未來該做
些什麼。文長約 120 個單詞（words）左右。

Renting a Car

It is late afternoon at Central Airport. This is a very busy time of day. Several flights have just landed. Many of the arriving passengers want to rent a car. Most choose Alamo because the prices are low. The clerks are trying to serve several people at the same time.

Unfortunately, there will not be enough cars for everyone. The woman standing in line will not be able to rent a car from Alamo. The clerks will try to help her find another car at a different company. She will rent one from National but she will have to pay more. *Next time* she will remember to reserve a car in advance. It will save her a lot of time and trouble.

3. Renting a Car

3. 租 車

It is late afternoon at Central Airport.

現在是傍晚時分的中央機場。

This is a very busy time of day.

這是一天中非常忙碌的時刻。

Several flights have just landed.

有許多班機剛降落。

Many of the arriving passengers want to rent a car.

許多抵達的乘客想要租車。

Most choose Alamo because the prices are low.

大部份的人選擇阿拉莫，因爲價格較低。

The clerks are trying to serve several people at the same time.

店員試著同時服務好幾個人。

** ———————————————

rent〔rɛnt〕v. 租　　late〔let〕adj. 晚的
central〔'sɛntrəl〕adj. 中央的　　airport〔'ɛr,port〕n. 機場
several〔'sɛvərəl〕adj. 幾個的　　flight〔flaɪt〕n. 班機
land〔lænd〕v. 降落；著陸　　arrive〔ə'raɪv〕v. 抵達
passenger〔'pæsṇdʒɚ〕n. 乘客
choose〔tʃuz〕v. 選擇　　price〔praɪs〕n. 價格
low〔lo〕adj. 低的　　clerk〔klɝk〕n. 店員
serve〔sɝv〕v. 服務　　*at the same time* 同時

Unfortunately, there will not be enough cars for everyone.	不幸的是，這裡將沒有足夠的車給所有的人。
The woman standing in line will not be able to rent a car from Alamo.	那位排隊的女士將無法租到阿拉莫的車。
The clerks will try to help her find another car at a different company.	店員會試著幫她從另一間公司找另一輛車。
She will rent one from National but she will have to pay more.	她將從國際租一台車，但是她必須付更多錢。
Next time she will remember to reserve a car in advance.	下次，她會記得要事先預約租車。
It will save her a lot of time and trouble.	這樣可以讓她省下很多時間和麻煩。

** ———————————— —

unfortunately〔ʌnˈfɔrtʃənɪtlɪ〕*adv.* 不幸地
stand in line 排隊
company〔ˈkʌmpənɪ〕*n.* 公司
national〔ˈnæʃənl̩〕*adj.* 國際的
reserve〔rɪˈzɜv〕*v.* 預訂
in advance 事先   save〔sev〕*v.* 節省
trouble〔ˈtrʌbl̩〕*n.* 麻煩

TEST 4

提 示

請根據下方圖片的場景，描述整個事件發生的前因後果。文章請分兩段，第一段說明之前發生了什麼事情，並根據圖片內容描述現在的狀況；第二段請合理說明接下來可能會發生什麼事，或者未來該做些什麼。文長約 120 個單詞（words）左右。

New Neighbors

The Smiths have just moved to a new house. It is a big house in a suburban area. Mrs. Smith sees some of her neighbors walking by with their dog. She says hello and the neighbors come to meet her. Mrs. Smith calls her family. Everyone gets to know one another.

One of the Smiths' neighbors, Mrs. Brown, invites them to dinner next week. They will go to the Browns' house on Saturday. They will learn a lot about their new neighborhood. They will also find out that they have a lot in common with the Browns. Everyone will have a good time, and they will all become close friends. The Smiths will feel at home in their new house.

4. New Neighbors

4. 新鄰居

The Smiths have just moved to a new house.

史密斯一家人剛搬進新家。

It is a big house in a suburban area.

那是在郊區的一幢大房子。

Mrs. Smith sees some of her neighbors walking by with their dog.

史密斯太太看到她的一些鄰居牽著狗經過。

She says hello and the neighbors come to meet her.

她打了聲招呼，而鄰居們便過來認識她。

Mrs. Smith calls her family.

史密斯太太叫喚她的家人。

Everyone gets to know one another.

大家就相互認識了。

** ————————————

neighbor〔'nebɚ〕n. 鄰居
move〔muv〕v. 搬家
suburban〔sə'bɝbən〕adj. 郊外的
area〔'ɛrɪə〕n. 地區   **walk by** 經過
say hello 打招呼   meet〔mit〕v. 認識
call〔kɔl〕v. 叫   **get to V.** 得以~

One of the Smiths' neighbors, Mrs. Brown, invites them to dinner next week.	史密斯家的其中一個鄰居伯朗太太，邀請他們下週吃晚餐。
They will go to the Browns' house on Saturday.	他們會在星期六到伯朗家。
They will learn a lot about their new neighborhood.	他們將會更了解附近的鄰居。
They will also find out that they have a lot in common with the Browns.	他們也會了解自己與伯朗家有很多共同點。
Everyone will have a good time, and they will all become close friends.	每個人都會玩得很愉快，而且他們都會成為親密的朋友。
The Smiths will feel at home in their new house.	史密斯一家人將會在新家過得很自在。

** ——————————————

invite〔ˈɪnvaɪt〕*v.* 邀請
neighborhood〔ˈnebɚˌhʊd〕*n.* 鄰近地區；附近的鄰居
find out 了解   common〔ˈkɑmən〕*adj.* 共同的
have a lot in common 有很多共同點
have a good time 玩得很愉快   close〔klos〕*adj.* 親密的
feel at home 覺得自在

TEST 5

提 示

請根據下方圖片的場景，描述整個事件發生的前因
後果。文章請分兩段，第一段說明之前發生了什麼
事情，並根據圖片內容描述現在的狀況；第二段請
合理說明接下來可能會發生什麼事，或者未來該做
些什麼。文長約 120 個單詞（words）左右。

Preparing a Special Meal

Thanksgiving is coming. Mrs. Smith plans to cook a big meal for her family. She goes to the supermarket to buy everything she needs. *In addition to* a turkey, she buys a lot of vegetables. She plans to make several different dishes. She will have to spend all day in the kitchen.

On Thanksgiving morning Mrs. Smith will wake up very early. The turkey has to cook for several hours so she will put it in the oven right away. *Then* she will prepare all of the other dishes. Her husband and children will help her with the cooking, and they will also help to prepare the table. *In the afternoon*, other relatives will begin to arrive. They will all enjoy a happy reunion.

5. **Preparing a Special Meal**　　5. 準備特別的一餐

Thanksgiving is coming.　　感恩節即將來臨。

Mrs. Smith plans to cook a
big meal for her family.
　　史密斯太太打算爲她的家
人煮一頓大餐。

She goes to the supermarket to
buy everything she needs.
　　她去超級市場買她所需的
一切。

In addition to a turkey, she
buys a lot of vegetables.
　　除了火雞之外,她買了很
多蔬菜。

She plans to make several
different dishes.
　　她打算做好幾道不同的菜。

She will have to spend all day
in the kitchen.
　　她將會在廚房裡花上一整
天的時間。

** ————————————————

prepare〔 prɪ'pɛr 〕*v.* 準備
special〔'spɛʃəl 〕*adj.* 特別的　　meal〔 mil 〕*n.* 一餐
Thanksgiving〔,θæŋks'gɪvɪŋ〕*n.* 感恩節
plan〔 plæn 〕*v.* 計劃;打算　　family〔'fæməlɪ 〕*n.* 家人
supermarket〔'supɚ,mɑrkɪt 〕*n.* 超級市場
in addition to 除了…之外　　turkey〔'tɝkɪ 〕*n.* 火雞
vegetable〔'vɛdʒtəbl̩ 〕*n.* 蔬菜　　dish〔 dɪʃ 〕*n.* 菜餚

On Thanksgiving morning Mrs.
　Smith will wake up very early.

在感恩節的早上，史密斯太
太將會起得很早。

The turkey has to cook for
　several hours so she will put
　it in the oven right away.

火雞必須花好幾個小時烹調，
所以她會立刻把火雞放進烤
箱裡。

Then she will prepare all of the
　other dishes.

接著她會準備所有其他的菜
餚。

Her husband and children will
　help her with the cooking, and
　they will also help to prepare
　the table.

她的丈夫和小孩會幫忙她做
菜，而他們也會幫忙準備開
飯。

In the afternoon, other relatives
　will begin to arrive.

到了下午，其他的親戚會開
始抵達。

They will all enjoy a happy
　reunion.

他們全都會享受這歡聚的時
刻。

** ———————————————

wake up 起床　　turkey〔'tɝkɪ〕*n.* 火雞
oven〔'ʌvən〕*n.* 烤箱　　*right away* 立刻
prepare the table 準備開飯
relative〔'rɛlətɪv〕*n.* 親戚　　arrive〔ə'raɪv〕*v.* 到達
reunion〔ri'junjən〕*n.* 重聚；團圓

TEST 6

提 示

請根據下方圖片的場景，描述整個事件發生的前因
後果。文章請分兩段，第一段說明之前發生了什麼
事情，並根據圖片內容描述現在的狀況；第二段請
合理說明接下來可能會發生什麼事，或者未來該做
些什麼。文長約 120 個單詞（words）左右。

The Big Race

Every year there is a big cycling race. It lasts for three days and passes through several cities. People come from miles around to watch it. *This year*, the race will pass through Centerville. The mayor has made a good plan for the race. He hopes that it will be a successful event.

Thousands of cycling fans come to Centerville to see the race. They stay in hotels, eat at restaurants, and buy souvenirs. They bring a lot of needed money to the small town. *Best of all*, the race goes very smoothly. There are no accidents and the crowd behaves well, cheering enthusiastically for their favorite. The race organizers say that they will definitely choose Centerville again next year.

6. The Big Race　　　　6. 大型競賽

Every year there is a big cycling race.	每年都會有一場單車競賽。
It lasts for three days and passes through several cities.	競賽持續三天，並經過好幾個城市。
People come from miles around to watch it.	方圓幾英里的人都來觀看比賽。

This year, the race will pass through Centerville.	今年，這場比賽會經過中央鎮。
The mayor has made a good plan for the race.	市長已經爲競賽做了很好的規劃。
He hopes that it will be a successful event.	他希望這次的活動能夠成功。

**　　**━━━━━━━━━━━━━━━━━━━━

race〔res〕*n.* 競賽；比賽

cycling〔'saɪklɪŋ〕*n.* 騎腳踏車　　last〔læst〕*v.* 持續

pass through 經過　　mile〔maɪl〕*n.* 英里

around〔ə'raʊnd〕*adv.* 四面八方　***miles around*** 方圓幾英里

mayor〔'meɚ〕*n.* 市長　　plan〔plæn〕*n.* 計畫；規畫

successful〔sək'sɛsfəl〕*adj.* 成功的

event〔ɪ'vɛnt〕*n.* (大型) 活動

Thousands of cycling fans come to Centerville to see the race.	數以千計的單車迷都來到中央鎮看比賽。
They stay in hotels, eat at restaurants, and buy souvenirs.	他們住在旅館、在餐廳用餐,並購買紀念品。
They bring a lot of needed money to the small town.	他們為小鎮帶來許多鎮民所需要的錢。
Best of all, the race goes very smoothly.	最棒的是,競賽進行得很順利。
There are no accidents and the crowd behaves well, cheering enthusiastically for their favorite.	沒有意外發生,而且群眾表現良好,為他們最喜愛的選手熱烈加油。
The race organizers say that they will definitely choose Centerville again next year.	競賽主辦者說,他們明年一定會再選擇中央鎮。

** ————————————————————

fan〔fæn〕*n.* 迷　　　stay〔ste〕*v.* 暫住
hotel〔hoˈtɛl〕*n.* 旅館　　souvenir〔ˌsuvəˈnɪr〕*n.* 紀念品
best of all 最棒的是　　go〔go〕*v.* 進展
smoothly〔ˈsmuðlɪ〕*adv.* 順利地
accident〔ˈæksədənt〕*n.* 意外　　crowd〔kraud〕*n.* 人群
behave〔bɪˈhev〕*v.* 表現;行為　　cheer〔tʃɪr〕*v.* 喝采;歡呼
enthusiastically〔ɪnˌθjuzɪˈæstɪklɪ〕*adv.* 熱烈地
favorite〔ˈfevrɪt〕*n.* 最喜愛的人或物
organizer〔ˈɔrgəˌnaɪzɚ〕*n.* 主辦者
definitely〔ˈdɛfənɪtlɪ〕*adv.* 一定

TEST 7

提 示

請根據下方圖片的場景，描述整個事件發生的前因
後果。文章請分兩段，第一段說明之前發生了什麼
事情，並根據圖片內容描述現在的狀況；第二段請
合理說明接下來可能會發生什麼事，或者未來該做
些什麼。文長約 120 個單詞（words）左右。

Skateboard Hero

Billy was very interested in skateboarding. He often went to the park to watch the older kids skateboard there. He begged his parents to buy one for him. *At last*, they did. Billy took it to the park and tried to ride it, but it was harder than he had thought. He kept falling off.

One of the other kids will notice his trouble. He'll offer to teach Billy. He'll give Billy lots of useful tips. *Best of all*, he won't laugh when Billy makes mistakes. All of this will give the little boy a lot of confidence. *Eventually*, thanks to his hero, he will be able to ride the skateboard.

7. Skateboard Hero

Billy was very interested in skateboarding.

He often went to the park to watch the older kids skateboard there.

He begged his parents to buy one for him.

At last, they did.

Billy took it to the park and tried to ride it, but it was harder than he had thought.

He kept falling off.

7. 滑板英雄

比利對滑板運動非常有興趣。

他常到公園去看其他較年長的孩子在那裡玩滑板。

他請求父母買滑板給他。

最後,他們買給他了。

比利帶著滑板到公園,試著站在上面滑行,但是這比他所想的還要困難。

他不斷地跌倒。

**

skateboard〔'sket,bɔrd〕*n.* 滑板　*v.* 用滑板滑行
hero〔'hɪro〕*n.* 英雄　　***be interested in*** 對…有興趣
skateboarding〔'sket,bɔrdɪŋ〕*n.* 滑板運動
beg〔bɛg〕*v.* 乞求　　***at last*** 最後
ride〔raɪd〕*v.* 站著滑行　　hard〔hɑrd〕*adj.* 困難的
keep〔kip〕*v.* 持續;不斷　　***fall off*** 跌倒

One of the other kids will notice his trouble.

其中一個孩子會注意到比利的問題。

He'll offer to teach Billy.

他會願意敎比利。

He'll give Billy lots of useful tips.

他會告訴比利很多有用的技巧。

Best of all, he won't laugh when Billy makes mistakes.

最棒的是，當比利犯錯時，他不會嘲笑。

All of this will give the little boy a lot of confidence.

這所有的一切將會給小男孩很大的信心。

Eventually, thanks to his hero, he will be able to ride the skateboard.

最後，因爲他的英雄的幫忙，他將能夠玩滑板。

** ————————————————

notice〔'notɪs〕*v.* 注意到
trouble〔'trʌbḷ〕*n.* 問題；困擾
offer to V. 願意…   useful〔'jusfəl〕*adj.* 有用的
tip〔tɪp〕*n.* 技巧   ***best of all*** 最棒的是
laugh〔læf〕*v.* 笑   mistake〔mə'stek〕*n.* 錯誤
confidence〔'kɑnfədəns〕*n.* 信心
eventually〔ɪ'vɛntʃʊəlɪ〕*adv.* 最後   ***thanks to*** 由於
be able to V. 能夠…

TEST 8

提 示

請根據下方圖片的場景，描述整個事件發生的前因後果。文章請分兩段，第一段說明之前發生了什麼事情，並根據圖片內容描述現在的狀況；第二段請合理說明接下來可能會發生什麼事，或者未來該做些什麼。文長約 120 個單詞（words）左右。

A Sunday Boat Ride

Susan, Ann, and John wanted to go out on Sunday. They argued about what to do. Susan wanted to go for a boat ride on the lake. *But* Ann is afraid of water, so she didn't want to go. John thought she should face her fear. *At last* they persuaded Ann to try.

At first, Ann will feel very nervous in the boat. *But* Susan and John will help her to relax. They will chat about many things and look at the nice scenery. *After about an hour* on the calm and beautiful lake, they will return to the shore. *Surprisingly*, Ann will feel sorry that the trip is over. She will ask Susan and John to join her at the lake next week.

8. A Sunday Boat Ride

8. 週日乘船

Susan, Ann, and John wanted to go out on Sunday.

蘇珊、安和約翰星期天想要出去。

They argued about what to do.

他們爭論著要做什麼。

Susan wanted to go for a boat ride on the lake.

蘇珊想要到湖上乘船。

But Ann is afraid of water, so she didn't want to go.

但是安怕水,所以她不想去。

John thought she should face her fear.

約翰覺得她應該要面對自己的恐懼。

At last they persuaded Ann to try.

最後,他們說服了安去嘗試。

** ────────────────

argue〔'ɑrgju〕*v.* 爭論　　lake〔lek〕*n.* 湖

be afraid of 害怕　　face〔fes〕*v.* 面對

fear〔fɪr〕*n.* 恐懼　　***at last*** 最後

persuade〔pə'swed〕*v.* 說服

At first, Ann will feel very nervous in the boat.	起初，安在船上會覺得非常緊張。
But Susan and John will help her to relax.	但是蘇珊和約翰會幫助她放鬆。
They will chat about many things and look at the nice scenery.	他們會聊很多事，並且欣賞美麗的風景。
After about an hour on the calm and beautiful lake, they will return to the shore.	在平靜美麗的湖上待大約一小時後，他們會回到岸邊。
Surprisingly, Ann will feel sorry that the trip is over.	令人驚訝的是，安會因為行程結束而感到可惜。
She will ask Susan and John to join her at the lake next week.	她將會邀請蘇珊和約翰下週和她一起來湖邊。

**

at first 起初　　nervous (ˈnɝvəs) adj. 緊張的
relax (rɪˈlæks) v. 放鬆　　chat (tʃæt) v. 聊天
scenery (ˈsinərɪ) n. 風景　　calm (kɑm) adj. 平靜的
return (rɪˈtɝn) v. 返回　　shore (ʃor) n. (海、湖、河的) 岸
surprisingly (səˈpraɪzɪŋlɪ) adv. 令人驚訝的是
sorry (ˈsɔrɪ) adj. 感到可惜的　　trip (trɪp) n. 旅程
join (dʒɔɪn) v. 加入；和…一起做同樣的事

TEST 9

提 示

請根據下方圖片的場景，描述整個事件發生的前因
後果。文章請分兩段，第一段說明之前發生了什麼
事情，並根據圖片內容描述現在的狀況；第二段請
合理說明接下來可能會發生什麼事，或者未來該做
些什麼。文長約 120 個單詞（words）左右。

The Road to Fame

Jack and his friends like to play music. Each of them can play a different instrument. They often practice together and dream of becoming famous. *However*, no one will hire them. *One day*, they decide to practice on the street instead of at Jack's house. They take their instruments and go downtown.

As they play, some passersby will stop to listen while others will just ignore them. *Surprisingly*, some people will give them money. They will drop coins and even bills in the instrument cases. Encouraged by this, Jack and his friends will try hard to play even better. They will go back to the street corner every weekend. *Eventually*, they will become well known to everyone in the neighborhood— famous at last!

9. **The Road to Fame**   9. 成名之路

Jack and his friends like to play music.	傑克和他的朋友喜歡演奏音樂。
Each of them can play a different instrument.	他們每個人都會演奏不同的樂器。
They often practice together and dream of becoming famous.	他們常常一起練習,並夢想能夠成名。

However, no one will hire them.	然而,沒有人要雇用他們。
One day, they decide to practice on the street instead of at Jack's house.	有一天,他們決定在街上練習,而不是在傑克家。
They take their instruments and go downtown.	他們帶著自己的樂器到市中心。

** ————————————————————

road〔rod〕*n.* 道路　　fame〔fem〕*n.* 名聲
play〔ple〕*v.* 演奏
instrument〔'ɪnstrəmənt〕*n.* 樂器 (= *musical instrument*)
practice〔'præktɪs〕*v.* 練習　　***dream of*** 夢想;幻想
famous〔'feməs〕*adj.* 有名的　　hire〔haɪr〕*v.* 雇用
one day 有一天　　decide〔dɪ'saɪd〕*v.* 決定
instead of 而不是　　downtown〔'daʊn'taʊn〕*adv.* 到市中心

As they play, some passersby will stop to listen while others will just ignore them.	當他們演奏時，有些行人會停下來聆聽，而有些人則是忽略他們。
Surprisingly, some people will give them money.	令人驚訝的是，有些人會給他們錢。
They will drop coins and even bills in the instrument cases.	他們會在樂器箱裡投下硬幣，甚至是紙鈔。
Encouraged by this, Jack and his friends will try hard to play even better.	受到這件事的鼓勵，傑克和他的朋友會努力，想要表演得更好。
They will go back to the street corner every weekend.	他們會每個週末都回到街角。
Eventually, they will become well known to everyone in the neighborhood—famous at last!	最後，他們在這個社區會變得家喻戶曉——最後成名！

** ─────────────────

passersby〔'pæsɚs'baɪ〕*n. pl.* 行人【單數形是 passeɪby】
while〔hwaɪl〕*conj.* 然而【表對比】　　ignore〔ɪg'nor〕*v.* 忽視
surprisingly〔sə'praɪzɪŋlɪ〕*adv.* 令人驚訝地
drop〔drɑp〕*v.* 投入　　coin〔kɔɪn〕*n.* 硬幣　　bill〔bɪl〕*n.* 紙鈔
case〔kes〕*n.* 箱子　　encourage〔ɪn'kɝɪdʒ〕*v.* 鼓勵
hard〔hɑrd〕*adv.* 努力地　　corner〔'kɔrnɚ〕*n.* 角落
weekend〔'wik'ɛnd〕*n.* 週末　　eventually〔ɪ'vɛntʃʊəlɪ〕*adv.* 最後
be well known to sb. 是某人所熟知的
neighborhood〔'nebɚ,hʊd〕*n.* 鄰近地區　　***at last*** 最後；終於

TEST 10

提示

請根據下方圖片的場景，描述整個事件發生的前因後果。文章請分兩段，第一段說明之前發生了什麼事情，並根據圖片內容描述現在的狀況；第二段請合理說明接下來可能會發生什麼事，或者未來該做些什麼。文長約 120 個單詞（words）左右。

Three Heads Are Better than One

Greg is a manager at XYZ Company. He is responsible for writing many reports about the company's expenses. *One day*, he was checking a report. He found that something was wrong. The numbers just didn't add up. He couldn't figure out what the problem was; therefore, he asked his colleagues to help.

Mary and Pete will look over the report carefully. *At first*, they will not be able to see anything wrong, either. *Then, suddenly*, one of them will find the error. *Once* they know what the problem is, they will all work together to solve it. Greg will thank the others for their help, but both Mary and Pete will say to forget it. *After all*, that's what friends are for.

10. **Three Heads**
Are Better than One

10. 三個臭皮匠
勝過一個諸葛亮

Greg is a manager at XYZ Company.

葛列格是 XYZ 公司的經理。

He is responsible for writing many reports about the company's expenses.

他負責撰寫公司許多開支的報告。

One day, he was checking a report.

有一天，他正在檢查報告。

He found that something was wrong.

他發現有些不對勁。

The numbers just didn't add up.

數字不合理。

He couldn't figure out what the problem was; therefore, he asked his colleagues to help.

他無法想出問題在哪，因此，他請同事幫忙。

** ———————————————

本文的標題源自諺語：*Two heads are better than one.*
（三個臭皮匠勝過一個諸葛亮）

manager (ˈmænɪdʒɚ) *n.* 經理　　company (ˈkʌmpənɪ) *n.* 公司
be responsible for 負責　　report (rɪˈport) *n.* 報告
expense (ɪkˈspɛns) *n.* 費用；花費　　check (tʃɛk) *v.* 檢查
number (ˈnʌmbɚ) *n.* 數字　　***add up*** 合計；合理；有道理
figure out 想出；了解　　problem (ˈprɑbləm) *n.* 問題
colleague (ˈkɑlig) *n.* 同事 (= *co-worker*)

Mary and Pete will look over
the report carefully.

瑪麗和彼特會仔細地檢查
報告。

At first, they will not be able to
see anything wrong, either.

一開始，他們也無法看出
任何問題。

Then, suddenly, one of them
will find the error.

然後，突然間，其中一個
人會發現錯誤。

Once they know what the
problem is, they will all work
together to solve it.

當他們一發現問題，他們
將會合作來解決。

Greg will thank the others for
their help, but both Mary and
Pete will say to forget it.

葛列格會感謝他們的幫忙，
但是瑪麗和彼特都會說不
用道謝。

After all, that's what friends
are for.

畢竟，朋友就是該互相幫
忙。

**

look over 仔細檢查　　carefully〔'kɛrfəlɪ〕*adv.* 仔細地

at first 起初；一開始　　either〔'iðɚ〕*adv.* 也【用於否定句】

suddenly〔'sʌdn̩lɪ〕*adv.* 突然地　　error〔'ɛrɚ〕*n.* 錯誤

work together 合作　　solve〔salv〕*v.* 解決

forget it 算了；沒關係；別再提了　　*after all* 畢竟

That's what friends are for. 那就是朋友的用處；朋友就是
　　該互相幫忙。

TEST 11

提 示

請根據下方圖片的場景,描述整個事件發生的前因
後果。文章請分兩段,第一段說明之前發生了什麼
事情,並根據圖片內容描述現在的狀況;第二段請
合理說明接下來可能會發生什麼事,或者未來該做
些什麼。文長約 120 個單詞(words)左右。

Andrew's New Job

Andrew was out of work. He applied to many companies, but no one wanted to hire him. He finally found a job as a salesman. He makes no salary, but he earns a commission on every sale. He works very hard at it. He just hopes he can make ends meet.

Although he has no sales experience, Andrew is good at his job. People like him and trust him. They buy many of the company's products from him. He will not only make a lot of money this year, but be named the Salesman of the Year in his company. *Because of this*, his boss will notice him and give him a promotion. It proves that hard work pays off.

11. Andrew's New Job　　11. 安德魯的新工作

Andrew was out of work.

安德魯失業了。

He applied to many companies, but no one wanted to hire him.

他應徵了很多間公司，但是沒有一間想雇用他。

He finally found a job as a salesman.

他最後找到一份業務員的工作。

He makes no salary, but he earns a commission on every sale.

他沒有底薪，但是每一筆生意他都可以抽取佣金。

He works very hard at it.

他非常努力工作。

He just hopes he can make ends meet.

他只希望可以勉強糊口。

**　**

------

job〔dʒɑb〕n. 工作　　***out of work*** 失業的
apply〔ə'plaɪ〕v. 申請；應徵　　company〔'kʌmpənɪ〕n. 公司
hire〔haɪr〕v. 雇用　　finally〔'faɪnḷɪ〕adv. 最後；終於
salesman〔'selzmən〕n. 推銷員；業務員
salary〔'sælərɪ〕n. 薪水　　earn〔ɝn〕v. 賺（錢）
commission〔kə'mɪʃən〕n. 佣金
sale〔sel〕n. 銷售；交易　　hard〔hɑrd〕adv. 努力地
make ends meet 使收支相抵；勉強糊口（= *make both ends meet*）

Although he has no sales experience, Andrew is good at his job.	雖然安德魯沒有銷售經驗，但是他很擅長這份工作。
People like him and trust him.	人們喜歡並且信賴他。
They buy many of the company's products from him.	他們向他購買該公司的許多產品。

He will not only make a lot of money this year, but be named the Salesman of the Year in his company.	他今年將不僅會賺很多錢，也會被提名爲公司的年度業務員。
Because of this, his boss will notice him and give him a promotion.	因爲如此，他的老闆將會注意到他，並讓他升遷。
It proves that hard work pays off.	這證明了努力是會有收穫的。

**

although〔ɔl'ðo〕*conj.* 雖然　　sales〔selz〕*adj.* 銷售的
experience〔ɪk'spɪrɪəns〕*n.* 經驗　　*be good at* 擅長
trust〔trʌst〕*v.* 信任　　product〔'prɑdəkt〕*n.* 產品
not only…but (*also*)~ 不僅…而且~　　*make money* 賺錢
name〔nem〕*v.* 提名　　boss〔bɔs〕*n.* 老闆
notice〔'notɪs〕*v.* 注意到　　promotion〔prə'moʃən〕*n.* 升遷
prove〔pruv〕*v.* 證明　　*pay off* 有利可圖；沒有白費

TEST 12

提 示

請根據下方圖片的場景，描述整個事件發生的前因
後果。文章請分兩段，第一段說明之前發生了什麼
事情，並根據圖片內容描述現在的狀況；第二段請
合理說明接下來可能會發生什麼事，或者未來該做
些什麼。文長約 120 個單詞（words）左右。

The Smoking Break

Gloria works in a big office building.
No one is allowed to smoke in the building.
Therefore, the employees must go outside
to enjoy a cigarette. Gloria does this four
times a day every day. She takes a break
of ten minutes on the sidewalk outside her
building. It is part of her routine.

In fact, Gloria gave up smoking several
months ago. *But* she found that she enjoyed
going outside on her breaks. *Now* she sits
beside the building and chats on the phone
or reads a magazine. She enjoys the fresh
air and sunshine. Everyone tells her that
smoking is bad for her, but Gloria just
smiles. She has given up smoking, but she
will never give up her smoking breaks!

12. **The Smoking Break**　　12. 抽煙時間

Gloria works in a big office building.

葛蘿莉亞在一間辦公大樓上班。

No one is allowed to smoke in the building.

沒有人可以在大樓內抽煙。

Therefore, the employees must go outside to enjoy a cigarette.

因此，員工必須到外面去抽煙。

Gloria does this four times a day every day.

葛蘿莉亞每天都出去外面抽煙四次。

She takes a break of ten minutes on the sidewalk outside her building.

她在大樓外的人行道上休息十分鐘。

It is part of her routine.

這是她例行公事的一部份。

** ─────────────

smoking〔'smokɪŋ〕*n.* 抽煙　　break〔brɛk〕*n.* 休息時間
office building 辦公大樓　　allow〔ə'laʊd〕*v.* 允許
smoke〔smok〕*v.* 抽煙　　employee〔ˌɛmplɔɪ'i〕*n.* 員工
outside〔'aʊt'saɪd〕*prep.* 在…外面
cigarette〔ˌsɪgə'rɛt〕*n.* 香煙　　time〔taɪm〕*n.* 次數
take a break 休息　　sidewalk〔'saɪdˌwɔk〕*n.* 人行道
routine〔ru'tin〕*n.* 例行公事

In fact, Gloria gave up smoking several months ago.

事實上，葛蘿莉亞幾個月前戒煙了。

But she found that she enjoyed going outside on her breaks.

但是她發現自己喜歡在休息時走到外面。

Now she sits beside the building and chats on the phone or reads a magazine.

現在她坐在大樓旁邊，並用電話聊天或看雜誌。

She enjoys the fresh air and sunshine.

她喜歡新鮮的空氣和陽光。

Everyone tells her that smoking is bad for her, but Gloria just smiles.

每個人都告訴她抽煙對她不好，但是葛蘿莉亞都微笑以對。

She has given up smoking, but she will never give up her smoking breaks!

她已經戒煙了，但是她永遠不會戒掉她的抽煙時間！

** ———————————————

in fact 事實上   *give up* 放棄
give up smoking 戒煙 (*= quit smoking*)
beside〔bɪˈsaɪd〕*prep.* 在…的旁邊   chat〔tʃæt〕*v.* 閒聊
magazine〔ˈmæɡəˌzin〕*n.* 雜誌   fresh〔frɛʃ〕*adj.* 新鮮的
air〔ɛr〕*n.* 空氣   sunshine〔ˈsʌnˌʃaɪn〕*n.* 陽光

TEST 13

提 示

請根據下方圖片的場景，描述整個事件發生的前因
後果。文章請分兩段，第一段說明之前發生了什麼
事情，並根據圖片內容描述現在的狀況；第二段請
合理說明接下來可能會發生什麼事，或者未來該做
些什麼。文長約 120 個單詞（words）左右。

The Parade

Every Thanksgiving there is a big parade in New York. There are lots of floats and marching bands. The bands come from all over the country. Only the best high school bands are invited. *This year*, Central High School was chosen for the parade. All of the students are excited but a little nervous.

Despite their nervousness, they will perform well in the parade. They will even be on TV! All of their friends and family at home will cheer when they see them. *After the parade*, the students will go on a tour of the city. They will visit the Statue of Liberty and a museum. They will have a lot to talk about when they go home.

13. **The Parade**　　　　13. 遊　行

Every Thanksgiving there is a big parade in New York.	每年的感恩節，紐約都會有盛大的遊行。
There are lots of floats and marching bands.	有許多的遊行花車和軍樂隊。
The bands come from all over the country.	這些樂隊來自全國各地。

Only the best high school bands are invited.	只有最好的高中樂隊才會受邀。
This year, Central High School was chosen for the parade.	今年，中央高級中學獲選參與遊行。
All of the students are excited but a little nervous.	全部的學生都很興奮，而且有點緊張。

** ——————————————

parade〔pə'red〕*n.* 遊行
Thanksgiving〔ˏθæŋks'gɪvɪŋ〕*n.* 感恩節
float〔flot〕*n.*（遊行時用的）花車
march〔mɑrtʃ〕*v.* 行軍　　　band〔bænd〕*n.* 樂隊
marching band 軍樂隊　　***all over the country*** 全國各地
invite〔ɪn'vaɪt〕*v.* 邀請　　central〔'sɛntrəl〕*adj.* 中央的
choose〔tʃuz〕*v.* 選擇　　excited〔ɪk'saɪtɪd〕*adj.* 興奮的
nervous〔'nɜvəs〕*adj.* 緊張的

Despite their nervousness,
　they will perform well in
　the parade.

儘管他們很緊張，他們還是
會在遊行中表現良好。

They will even be on TV!

他們甚至會上電視！

All of their friends and family
　at home will cheer when
　they see them.

他們所有在家裡的朋友和家
人，看到他們時都會歡呼。

After the parade, the students
　will go on a tour of the city.

遊行過後，學生們會遊覽城
市。

They will visit the Statue of
　Liberty and a museum.

他們會參觀自由女神像和博
物館。

They will have a lot to talk
　about when they go home.

當他們回家時，將會有很多
事情可以談論。

** ───────────────

despite〔dɪ'spaɪt〕*prep.* 儘管 (= *in spite of*)
nervousness〔'nɜvəsnɪs〕*n.* 緊張
perform〔pɚ'fɔrm〕*v.* 表演
cheer〔tʃɪr〕*v.* 歡呼　　***go on a tour*** 去遊覽
visit〔'vɪzɪt〕*v.* 參觀　　statue〔'stætʃʊ〕*n.* 雕像
liberty〔'lɪbɚtɪ〕*n.* 自由
the Statue of Liberty 自由女神像
museum〔mju'ziəm〕*n.* 博物館

TEST 14

提 示

請根據下方圖片的場景，描述整個事件發生的前因後果。文章請分兩段，第一段說明之前發生了什麼事情，並根據圖片內容描述現在的狀況；第二段請合理說明接下來可能會發生什麼事，或者未來該做些什麼。文長約 120 個單詞（words）左右。

A Kind Stranger

Gary is from Singapore. He decided to visit Taipei on his vacation. He was very excited about seeing Taipei 101. *However*, he had trouble getting around because he is not familiar with Taipei. He couldn't find the right bus stop. *Finally*, he asked a passerby for help.

The young woman will help him get to his destination. She will take him to the correct bus stop and read the information signs with him. They will find a bus that goes directly to Taipei 101. Gary will enjoy his visit there very much. He will always remember the view of Taipei from the top. He will also remember the kindness of the young woman that helped him.

14. A Kind Stranger

14. 親切的陌生人

Gary is from Singapore.

蓋瑞來自新加坡。

He decided to visit Taipei on his vacation.

他決定在放假時來台北。

He was very excited about seeing Taipei 101.

他對於可以看到台北101感到很興奮。

However, he had trouble getting around because he is not familiar with Taipei.

然而，因爲對台北不熟悉，他很難四處逛。

He couldn't find the right bus stop.

他無法找到正確的公車站。

Finally, he asked a passerby for help.

最後，他請一個路人幫忙。

** ─────────────

kind〔kaɪnd〕*adj.* 親切的；好心的
stranger〔'strendʒɚ〕*n.* 陌生人
Singapore〔'sɪŋgəˌpor〕*n.* 新加坡
visit〔'vɪzɪt〕*v.* 參觀　　vacation〔ve'keʃən〕*n.* 假期
building〔'bɪldɪŋ〕*n.* 大樓　　trouble〔'trʌbḷ〕*n.* 困難
have trouble + V-ing 做…有困難　　***get around*** 到處走走
familiar〔fə'mɪljɚ〕*adj.* 熟悉的　　***bus stop*** 公車站
finally〔'faɪnḷɪ〕*adv.* 最後
passerby〔'pæsɚ'baɪ〕*n.* 過路人；行人

The young woman will help him get to his destination.

那位小姐會幫助他到達目的地。

She will take him to the correct bus stop and read the information signs with him.

她會帶他到正確的公車站，並和他一起看站牌上的資訊。

They will find a bus that goes directly to Taipei 101.

他們會找到一台直達台北101的公車。

Gary will enjoy his visit there very much.

蓋瑞會很喜歡在那裡遊覽。

He will always remember the view of Taipei from the top.

他會永遠記得從頂端看台北的景色。

He will also remember the kindness of the young woman that helped him.

他也會永遠記得那位幫助過他的親切的小姐。

**

get to 到達　　destination〔͵dɛstə'neʃən〕*n.* 目的地
correct〔kə'rɛkt〕*adj.* 正確的
information〔͵ɪnfɚ'meʃən〕*n.* 資訊
sign〔saɪn〕*n.* 告示牌　　directly〔də'rɛktlɪ〕*adv.* 直接地
visit〔'vɪzɪt〕*n.* 參觀；遊覽　　view〔vju〕*n.* 景色
top〔tɑp〕*n.* 頂端　　kindness〔'kaɪndnɪs〕*n.* 親切的行為

TEST 15

提 示

請根據下方圖片的場景,描述整個事件發生的前因
後果。文章請分兩段,第一段說明之前發生了什麼
事情,並根據圖片內容描述現在的狀況;第二段請
合理說明接下來可能會發生什麼事,或者未來該做
些什麼。文長約 120 個單詞(words)左右。

A New Career

Bob worked in an automobile factory. He made a good living there, but then the company went out of business. *Suddenly*, Bob had no job. He decided to try something new. He opened a hot dog stand at a popular beach. His delicious hot dogs were very popular with people.

Word will spread about Bob's good hot dogs. More and more people will come to eat them. *Soon* he will have to hire someone to help him. *Then* he will open a small restaurant so that he can sell more hot dogs. This will also be very successful, and he will have to open an even bigger restaurant. *Soon* Bob will have a whole new career in the restaurant business.

15. A New Career

15. 新的職業

Bob worked in an automobile factory.

鮑伯在一間汽車工廠工作。

He made a good living there, but then the company went out of business.

他在那裡的待遇不錯，但是後來工廠卻倒閉了。

Suddenly, Bob had no job.

突然間，鮑伯失業了。

He decided to try something new.

他決定嘗試一些新事物。

He opened a hot dog stand at a popular beach.

他在熱鬧的海邊開了一間熱狗攤。

His delicious hot dogs were very popular with people.

他美味可口的熱狗非常受人歡迎。

**

career〔kə'rɪr〕n. 職業　　automobile〔'ɔtəmə‚bil〕n. 汽車
factory〔'fæktrɪ〕n. 工廠　　*make a living* 謀生
make a good living 過舒適的生活
go out of business 倒閉　　suddenly〔'sʌdn̩lɪ〕adv. 突然地
open〔'opən〕v. 使（商店）開張　　*hot dog* 熱狗
stand〔stænd〕n. 攤子　　beach〔bitʃ〕n. 海邊
delicious〔dɪ'lɪʃəs〕adj. 美味的
be popular with 受…歡迎

Word will spread about Bob's
good hot dogs.

關於鮑伯好吃的熱狗的傳
聞將流傳開來。

More and more people will
come to eat them.

會有越來越多人來吃。

Soon he will have to hire
someone to help him.

很快地，他將必須雇人來
幫忙。

Then he will open a small
restaurant so that he can sell
more hot dogs.

接著他會開一間小餐廳，
如此一來他就可以賣更多
熱狗。

This will also be very
successful, and he will have
to open an even bigger
restaurant.

小餐廳也會非常成功，而
他必須開更大間的餐廳。

Soon Bob will have a whole
new career in the restaurant
business.

很快的，鮑伯將會在餐飲
業擁有全新的事業。

** ——————————————————————

word ﹝ wɜd ﹞ *n.* 話   spread ﹝ sprɛd ﹞ *v.* 流傳
hire ﹝ haɪr ﹞ *v.* 雇用   *so that* 以便於
successful ﹝ sək'sɛsfəl ﹞ *adj.* 成功的
whole new 全新的   *restaurant business* 餐飲業

TEST 16

提示

請根據下方圖片的場景，描述整個事件發生的前因後果。文章請分兩段，第一段說明之前發生了什麼事情，並根據圖片內容描述現在的狀況；第二段請合理說明接下來可能會發生什麼事，或者未來該做些什麼。文長約 120 個單詞（words）左右。

A Thrilling Ride

John took his daughter Jenny to an amusement park. She went to the park, but she refused to go on the rides. She did not want to ride anything that goes too fast. Her father wants her to be braver. He insisted on taking her on a spinning ride. *Reluctantly*, she agreed.

When the ride begins, she will feel nervous. Her father will smile at her and hold her hand. The ride will go faster and faster and Jenny will feel the wind rushing past her face. She will realize it is fun and start to laugh. *But* her father will hold her hand harder and harder. *When* she looks at him, she will see he is terrified and ready to scream.

16. A Thrilling Ride

16. 刺激的遊樂設施

John took his daughter Jenny to an amusement park.

約翰帶他的女兒珍妮到遊樂場。

She went to the park, but she refused to go on the rides.

她到了遊樂場，但是她拒絕坐遊樂設施。

She did not want to ride anything that goes too fast.

她不想坐任何開得太快的遊樂設施。

Her father wants her to be braver.

她的父親想要她更勇敢。

He insisted on taking her on a spinning ride.

他堅持帶她坐會旋轉的遊樂設施。

Reluctantly, she agreed.

她很不情願地同意了。

** ─────────

thrilling〔ˈθrɪlɪŋ〕*adj.* 刺激的　　ride〔raɪd〕*n.* 遊樂設施
amusement〔əˈmjuzmənt〕*n.* 娛樂
amusement park 遊樂場　　refuse〔rɪˈfjuz〕*v.* 拒絕
brave〔brev〕*adj.* 勇敢的
insist〔ɪnˈsɪst〕*v.* 堅持　　spin〔spɪn〕*v.* 旋轉
reluctantly〔rɪˈlʌktəntlɪ〕*adv.* 不情願地
agree〔əˈgri〕*v.* 同意

When the ride begins, she will feel nervous.

當遊樂設施啓動時，她會覺得很緊張。

Her father will smile at her and hold her hand.

她的父親會對她微笑，並握著她的手。

The ride will go faster and faster and Jenny will feel the wind rushing past her face.

這個遊樂設施的速度將會越來越快，而珍妮將會感受到風衝過她的臉頰。

She will realize it is fun and start to laugh.

她會發現這很有趣，並開始大笑。

But her father will hold her hand harder and harder.

但是她父親會把她的手握得越來越緊。

When she looks at him, she will see he is terrified and ready to scream.

當她看他時，她將會看到他非常害怕，並且準備尖叫。

***

**

nervous (ˈnɜvəs) *adj.* 緊張的　　hold (hold) *v.* 握住

wind (wɪnd) *n.* 風　　rush (rʌʃ) *v.* 衝

past (pæst) *prep.* 經過

realize (ˈriəˌlaɪz) *v.* 了解；知道

fun (fʌn) *adj.* 有趣的　　terrify (ˈtɛrəˌfaɪ) *v.* 使驚嚇

ready (ˈrɛdɪ) *adj.* 準備好的　　scream (skrim) *v.* 尖叫

TEST 17

提 示

　　請根據下方圖片的場景，描述整個事件發生的前因後果。文章請分兩段，第一段說明之前發生了什麼事情，並根據圖片內容描述現在的狀況；第二段請合理說明接下來可能會發生什麼事，或者未來該做些什麼。文長約 120 個單詞（words）左右。

The Amazing Juggler

Jack wanted to make some extra money. He could juggle pretty well, so he did it at a popular tourist place. People were impressed and gave him money. *But later* they got bored with his act. He made it more exciting by juggling fire. He kept adding new tricks to keep people interested.

Jack has become famous among the tourists. *Eventually* the owner of a circus will hear about him and offer Jack a job. He will travel with the circus for several months and see many interesting places. *Then* a television producer will come to the circus and be amazed by Jack. He will put him on TV, and this will make Jack world-famous. His part-time job will become his career.

17. The Amazing Juggler

Jack wanted to make some extra money.

He could juggle pretty well, so he did it at a popular tourist place.

People were impressed and gave him money.

But later they got bored with his act.

He made it more exciting by juggling fire.

He kept adding new tricks to keep people interested.

17. 驚人的雜耍表演者

傑克想賺些外快。

他非常會耍把戲,所以他在熱門的旅遊景點表演。

人們對他印象深刻,並給他錢。

但是後來他們就對他的表演厭煩了。

他為了讓表演看起來更刺激,所以就用火來耍把戲。

他不斷地增加新把戲,使觀眾一直很有興趣。

** ———————————

amazing〔ə'mezɪŋ〕adj. 驚人的
juggler〔'dʒʌglɚ〕n. 耍把戲的人　　extra〔'ɛkstrə〕adj. 額外的
pretty〔'prɪtɪ〕adv. 相當　　popular〔'pɑpjəlɚ〕adj. 熱門的
tourist〔'turɪst〕adj. 旅遊的
impressed〔ɪm'prɛst〕adj. 印象深刻的
bored〔bord〕adj. 厭倦的　　act〔ækt〕n. 表演
exciting〔ɪk'saɪtɪŋ〕adj. 刺激的
juggle〔'dʒʌgl〕v. 耍…;以…變戲法　　add〔æd〕v. 增加
trick〔trɪk〕n. 把戲　　interested〔'ɪntrɪstɪd〕adj. 有興趣的

Jack has become famous among the tourists.	傑克在遊客之間變得很有名。
Eventually the owner of a circus will hear about him and offer Jack a job.	最後，馬戲團老闆會聽聞他的名聲，並給傑克一份工作。
He will travel with the circus for several months and see many interesting places.	他將會隨著馬戲團旅行好幾個月，並遊覽許多有趣的地方。
Then a television producer will come to the circus and be amazed by Jack.	然後會有電視製作人來馬戲團，並對傑克的表演感到驚訝。
He will put him on TV, and this will make Jack world-famous.	他會讓他上電視，而這將會讓傑克聞名於世。
His part-time job will become his career.	他的兼職工作將會成為他的事業。

** ————————————

famous〔ˋfeməs〕*adj.* 有名的　　among〔əˋmʌŋ〕*prep.* 在…之中
eventually〔ɪˋvɛntʃʊəlɪ〕*adv.* 最後　　owner〔ˋonɚ〕*n.* 老闆
circus〔ˋsɝkəs〕*n.* 馬戲團　　***hear about*** 聽說關於…的事
offer〔ˋɔfɚ〕*v.* 提供　　travel〔ˋtrævl̩〕*v.* 旅行
producer〔prəˋdjusɚ〕*n.* 製作人　　amaze〔əˋmez〕*v.* 使驚訝
world-famous 舉世聞名的　　part-time〔ˋpartˋtaɪm〕*adj.* 兼職的
career〔kəˋrɪr〕*n.* 職業；事業

TEST 18

提 示

　　請根據下方圖片的場景，描述整個事件發生的前因
後果。文章請分兩段，第一段說明之前發生了什麼
事情，並根據圖片內容描述現在的狀況；第二段請
合理說明接下來可能會發生什麼事，或者未來該做
些什麼。文長約 120 個單詞（words）左右。

A Trip to San Francisco

The Jones family took a trip to San Francisco. They wanted to see all of the city sights. They don't have a car, so they had to use public transportation. *But* that was a lot of fun. They enjoyed riding the streetcar. It is not only transportation, but one of the tourist sights.

They will take the streetcar all the way to Fisherman's Wharf. It is one of the most famous attractions in San Francisco. They will walk along the pier and see lots of street performers. They will also find many good restaurants there. *After a delicious meal of fresh seafood*, they will get back on the streetcar. They will enjoy the ride back up the hills to their hotel.

18. A Trip to San Francisco   18. 舊金山之旅

The Jones family took a trip to San Francisco.

瓊斯一家人到舊金山玩。

They wanted to see all of the city sights.

他們想遊覽這個城市所有的景點。

They don't have a car, so they had to use public transportation.

他們沒有車，所以他們必須搭乘大眾運輸工具。

But that was a lot of fun.

但搭乘大眾運輸工具很好玩。

They enjoyed riding the streetcar.

他們很喜歡搭市區電車。

It is not only transportation, but one of the tourist sights.

那不僅是交通工具，也是觀光景點之一。

** ──────────

trip〔 trɪp 〕*n.* 旅行
San Francisco〔,sænfrən'sɪsko 〕*n.* 舊金山
family〔'fæməlɪ 〕*n.* 家人　　sight〔 saɪt 〕*n.* 景點；名勝
public〔'pʌblɪk 〕*adj.* 大眾的
transportation〔,trænspɚ'teʃən 〕*n.* 運輸工具
streetcar〔'strit,kɑr 〕*n.* 市區電車
not only…but（***also***）~　不僅…而且~
tourist〔'tʊrɪst 〕*adj.* 觀光的

They will take the streetcar all the way to Fisherman's Wharf.	他們將會搭乘市區電車一路到漁人碼頭。
It is one of the most famous attractions in San Francisco.	那是舊金山最有名的景點之一。
They will walk along the pier and see lots of street performers.	他們會沿著碼頭走，並看到很多街頭表演者。
They will also find many good restaurants there.	他們也會在那裡找到許多不錯的餐廳。
After a delicious meal of fresh seafood, they will get back on the streetcar.	在吃完一頓美味的新鮮海鮮餐後，他們會回到市區電車上。
They will enjoy the ride back up the hills to their hotel.	他們將會很喜愛搭乘市區電車回到在山丘上的飯店的這段路程。

**

all the way 一路　　fisherman〔'fɪʃəmən〕*n.* 漁夫
wharf〔hwɔrf〕*n.* 碼頭　　famous〔'feməs〕*adj.* 有名的
attraction〔ə'trækʃən〕*n.* 吸引人的事物；景點
along〔ə'lɔŋ〕*prep.* 沿著　　pier〔pɪr〕*n.* 碼頭
performer〔pə'fɔrmə〕*n.* 表演者
delicious〔dɪ'lɪʃəs〕*adj.* 美味的　　meal〔mil〕*n.* 一餐
fresh〔frɛʃ〕*adj.* 新鮮的　　seafood〔'si,fud〕*n.* 海鮮
hill〔hɪl〕*n.* 山丘；(道路的) 斜坡　　hotel〔ho'tɛl〕*n.* 飯店

TEST 19

提示

請根據下方圖片的場景,描述整個事件發生的前因
後果。文章請分兩段,第一段說明之前發生了什麼
事情,並根據圖片內容描述現在的狀況;第二段請
合理說明接下來可能會發生什麼事,或者未來該做
些什麼。文長約 120 個單詞(words)左右。

The Sun Artist

Center City is holding an art fair this week. Many painters, sculptors and other artists are displaying their work. John works with metal. He likes to make decorations, especially sun decorations. He brought many of his works of art to the fair. He set up a stall on the street.

Many customers will visit John's stall throughout the day. They will admire his artwork because it is unique; no other artist at the fair is selling anything like it. Some of them will buy a sun decoration for their home. John's prices are reasonable because he does not pursue art for money. He just likes making beautiful things. He plans to participate in the art fair again next year.

19. The Sun Artist

19. 太陽藝術家

Center City is holding an art fair this week.

這個星期，中央市正舉辦一場藝術博覽會。

Many painters, sculptors and other artists are displaying their work.

許多畫家、雕刻家和其他藝術家，都在這裡展示他們的作品。

John works with metal.

約翰是以金屬爲材料。

He likes to make decorations, especially sun decorations.

他喜歡做裝飾品，尤其是太陽飾品。

He brought many of his works of art to the fair.

他帶了許多自己的藝術品到博覽會來。

He set up a stall on the street.

他在街上設置了一個攤位。

**

artist (ˈɑrtɪst) *n.* 藝術家　　center (ˈsɛntɚ) *n.* 中央
hold (hold) *v.* 舉辦　　fair (fɛr) *n.* 博覽會；展示會
painter (ˈpentɚ) *n.* 畫家　　sculptor (ˈskʌlptɚ) *n.* 雕刻家
display (dɪˈsple) *v.* 展示；陳列
work (wɝk) *n.* 作品　　metal (ˈmɛtl̩) *n.* 金屬
decoration (ˌdɛkəˈreʃən) *n.* 裝飾品
especially (əˈspɛʃəlɪ) *adv.* 尤其　　*work of art* 藝術品
set up 設置　　stall (stɔl) *n.* 攤位

Many customers will visit John's stall throughout the day.

整天都會有許多顧客來參觀約翰的攤位。

They will admire his artwork because it is unique; no other artist at the fair is selling anything like it.

他們將會讚賞他的藝術品，因爲那很獨特；在博覽會上沒有其他藝術家銷售像這樣的東西。

Some of them will buy a sun decoration for their home.

有些人會買太陽飾品回家。

John's prices are reasonable because he does not pursue art for money.

約翰的價格很合理，因爲他不是爲了錢而從事藝術創作。

He just likes making beautiful things.

他只是喜歡製作漂亮的東西。

He plans to participate in the art fair again next year.

他打算明年再次參加藝術博覽會。

** ——————————

customer (ˈkʌstəmɚ) *n.* 顧客   visit (ˈvɪzɪt) *v.* 拜訪；參觀
throughout (θruˈaʊt) *prep.* 在…期間一直
admire (ədˈmaɪr) *v.* 讚賞   artwork (ˈɑrtˌwɜk) *n.* 藝術品
unique (juˈnik) *adj.* 獨特的   price (praɪs) *n.* 價格
reasonable (ˈriznəbl) *adj.* 合理的
pursue (pɚˈsu) *v.* 追求；從事   plan (plæn) *v.* 計畫；打算
participate (pɑrˈtɪsəˌpet) *v.* 參加 <*in*>

TEST 20

提 示

請根據下方圖片的場景,描述整個事件發生的前因
後果。文章請分兩段,第一段說明之前發生了什麼
事情,並根據圖片內容描述現在的狀況;第二段請
合理說明接下來可能會發生什麼事,或者未來該做
些什麼。文長約 120 個單詞(words)左右。

The Royal Guard

The Smiths went to London during their vacation. They saw many famous sights. They went to the Tower of London and Buckingham Palace. They especially wanted to see the Changing of the Guard. They waited outside the palace, but they were not there at the right time. They were so disappointed to miss it!

Fortunately, they saw a parade the next day. The Guards were marching in the parade! The Smiths ran to watch the parade and take a lot of pictures. They were very excited. *When* they get home, they will show the pictures to their friends and family. They will tell them all about the sights they saw in London and how impressive it was to see the Guards in person.

20. The Royal Guard

20. 皇家護衛隊

The Smiths went to London during their vacation.

史密斯一家人前往倫敦渡假。

They saw many famous sights.

他們參觀了許多有名的景點。

They went to the Tower of London and Buckingham Palace.

他們去了倫敦塔和白金漢宮。

They especially wanted to see the Changing of the Guard.

他們特別想看衛兵交接儀式。

They waited outside the palace, but they were not there at the right time.

他們在皇宮外面等待，但是他們去的時間不對。

They were so disappointed to miss it!

他們因為錯過這個儀式而非常失望！

** ─────────────

royal (ˈrɔɪəl) *adj.* 皇家的   guard (gɑrd) *n.* 守衛；護衛隊
London (ˈlʌndən) *n.* 倫敦   vacation (veˈkeʃən) *n.* 假期
famous (ˈfeməs) *adj.* 有名的   sight (saɪt) *n.* 景點
tower (ˈtaʊɚ) *n.* 塔   palace (ˈpælɪs) *n.* 皇宮
Buckingham Palace 白金漢宮
especially (əˈspɛʃəlɪ) *adv.* 尤其
right (raɪt) *adj.* 正確的；適當的
disappointed (ˌdɪsəˈpɔɪntɪd) *adj.* 失望的   miss (mɪs) *v.* 錯過

Fortunately, they saw a parade
the next day.

幸運的是，他們隔天看到了
遊行。

The Guards were marching in
the parade!

護衛隊在遊行中行軍！

The Smiths ran to watch the
parade and take a lot of
pictures.

史密斯一家人跑去看遊行，
並拍了很多照片。

They were very excited.

他們非常興奮。

When they get home, they will
show the pictures to their
friends and family.

當他們到家時，他們將會把
照片給朋友和家人看。

They will tell them all about
the sights they saw in London
and how impressive it was
to see the Guards in person.

他們會告訴他們關於在倫敦
看到的所有景點，和親眼看
到護衛隊是多麼地令人印象
深刻。

**　――――――――――――

　　fortunately〔'fɔrtʃənɪtlɪ〕*adv.* 幸運地
　　parade〔pə'red〕*n.* 遊行　　march〔martʃ〕*v.* 行軍
　　take a picture 拍照　　excited〔ɪk'saɪtɪd〕*adj.* 興奮的
　　show〔ʃo〕*v.* 把…給～看
　　impressive〔ɪm'prɛsɪv〕*adj.* 令人深刻印象的
　　in person 親自

TEST 21

提示

請根據下方圖片的場景,描述整個事件發生的前因後果。文章請分兩段,第一段說明之前發生了什麼事情,並根據圖片內容描述現在的狀況;第二段請合理說明接下來可能會發生什麼事,或者未來該做些什麼。文長約 120 個單詞(words)左右。

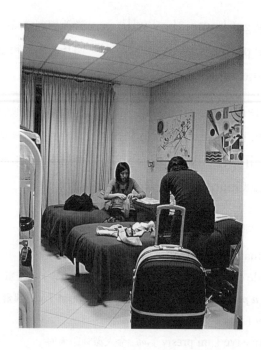

Early Morning Departure

Diane and her friend took a vacation together. They traveled around Europe for two weeks. *Now* it is time for them to go back home. Their flight leaves at 6:00 a.m. *Therefore*, they must be at the airport at 4:00 a.m. They had to get up very early—3:00!

Fortunately, they are staying close to the airport, so it won't take them long to get there. A taxi will pick them up at 3:30. They will hurriedly finish packing their bags and then go downstairs. There will be no time for breakfast until they get to the airport. *After* they check in, they will go to a coffee shop. *But* both of them will be too tired to eat anything!

21. Early Morning Departure   21. 一早離開

Diane and her friend took a vacation together.

黛安和她的朋友一起去渡假。

They traveled around Europe for two weeks.

她們在歐洲旅行了二週。

Now it is time for them to go back home.

現在是她們回家的時候了。

Their flight leaves at 6:00 a.m.

她們的班機是早上六點起飛。

Therefore, they must be at the airport at 4:00 a.m.

因此，她們必須早上四點就到機場。

They had to get up very early —3:00!

她們必須很早起來——三點！

**

departure〔dɪ'pɑrtʃɚ〕*n.* 出發
take a vacation 休假   travel〔'trævl〕*v.* 旅行
around〔ə'raʊnd〕*prep.* 在…到處
Europe〔'jʊrəp〕*n.* 歐洲   *it is time for~* 是該~的時間了
flight〔flaɪt〕*n.* 班機   leave〔liv〕*v.* 出發
airport〔'ɛr,port〕*n.* 機場   *get up* 起床

Fortunately, they are staying close to the airport, so it won't take them long to get there.

幸運的是，她們住在機場附近，所以到機場並不會花她們太長的時間。

A taxi will pick them up at 3:30.

計程車會在三點半來接她們。

They will hurriedly finish packing their bags and then go downstairs.

她們會匆促地打包完行李，然後下樓。

There will be no time for breakfast until they get to the airport.

直到到達機場，她們才有時間吃早餐。

After they check in, they will go to a coffee shop.

在辦好登機手續之後，她們會去咖啡店。

But both of them will be too tired to eat anything!

但是她們兩人將會累到沒有胃口吃任何東西！

**

fortunately (ˈfɔrtʃənɪtlɪ) *adv.* 幸運地
stay (ste) *v.* 暫住；投宿
close to 接近　　***pick up*** （開車）接（某人）
hurriedly (ˈhɜɪdlɪ) *adv.* 匆促地　　finish (ˈfɪnɪʃ) *v.* 結束；完成
pack (pæk) *v.* 打包　　bag (bæg) *n.* 行李
downstairs (ˈdaʊnˈstɛrz) *adv.* 到樓下　　***get to*** 到達
check in 辦理登機手續　　***coffee shop*** 咖啡店
too…to ~ 太…以致於不~　　tired (taɪrd) *adj.* 疲倦的

TEST 22

提 示

請根據右方圖片的場景，描述整個事件發生的前因
後果。文章請分兩段，第一段說明之前發生了什麼
事情，並根據圖片內容描述現在的狀況；第二段請
合理說明接下來可能會發生什麼事，或者未來該做
些什麼。文長約 120 個單詞（words）左右。

The Kind Guard

John is a foreigner who lives in Taipei. He had to go to a government building for some paperwork. *Unfortunately*, he had to wait a long time. He started to feel thirsty, so he looked for something to drink. He saw a vending machine. He wanted to buy something but didn't know how.

There is a security guard standing near John. He will notice his trouble and offer to help him. He will read the Chinese characters and show John which buttons to push. He will also give John the correct change. *At last*, John will get his drink, and he will thank the guard. He will be very impressed by the guard's kindness and feel better about having to wait so long.

22. The Kind Guard

22. 親切的警衛

John is a foreigner who lives in Taipei.

約翰是個住在台北的外國人。

He had to go to a government building for some paperwork.

他必須去政府大樓處理一些文書工作。

Unfortunately, he had to wait a long time.

不幸的是,他必須等很久。

He started to feel thirsty, so he looked for something to drink.

他開始覺得口渴,所以他就去找東西喝。

He saw a vending machine.

他看到一台販賣機。

He wanted to buy something but didn't know how.

他想買些東西,但他不知道如何操作。

**

kind〔kaɪnd〕*adj.* 親切的　　guard〔gɑrd〕*n.* 警衛
foreigner〔'fɔrɪnɚ〕*n.* 外國人
government〔'gʌvɚnmənt〕*n.* 政府　　building〔'bɪldɪŋ〕*n.* 大樓
paperwork〔'pepɚ,wɝk〕*n.* 文書工作
unfortunately〔ʌn'fɔrtʃənɪtlɪ〕*adv.* 不幸地
thirsty〔'θɝstɪ〕*adj.* 口渴的　　*look for* 尋找
vending machine 販賣機

There is a security guard standing near John.

有位保全人員站在約翰附近。

He will notice his trouble and offer to help him.

他會注意到他的困難並願意幫助他。

He will read the Chinese characters and show John which buttons to push.

他會唸出那些中文字並告訴約翰該按哪個按鈕。

He will also give John the correct change.

他也會給約翰正確的零錢。

At last, John will get his drink, and he will thank the guard.

最後，約翰會買到他的飲料，而他也會感謝那位警衛。

He will be very impressed by the guard's kindness and feel better about having to wait so long.

他將會對警衛的親切印象深刻，並且對於必須等這麼久感覺好多了。

** ——————————

security〔sɪ'kjʊrətɪ〕*n.* 安全　　***security guard*** 保全人員
notice〔'notɪs〕*v.* 注意到　　trouble〔'trʌbl̩〕*n.* 困擾；困難
offer〔'ɔfɚ〕*v.* 提供　　character〔'kærɪktɚ〕*n.* 文字
show〔ʃo〕*v.* 向…說明　　button〔'bʌtn̩〕*n.* 按鈕
push〔pʊʃ〕*v.* 按　　correct〔kə'rɛkt〕*adj.* 正確的
change〔tʃendʒ〕*n.* 零錢　　***at last*** 最後
drink〔drɪŋk〕*n.* 飲料　　***be impressed by*** 對～印象深刻
kindness〔'kaɪndnɪs〕*n.* 親切

TEST 23

提示

請根據下方圖片的場景，描述整個事件發生的前因
後果。文章請分兩段，第一段說明之前發生了什麼
事情，並根據圖片內容描述現在的狀況；第二段請
合理說明接下來可能會發生什麼事，或者未來該做
些什麼。文長約 120 個單詞（words）左右。

A Family Outing

The Bakers are a family of four. John and Mary have two children—Susan and Amy. Susan is eager to go to an amusement park. Her parents think it is not a good idea because Amy is too young. *But* Susan promises to help take care of her. *At last,* her parents agree.

The family will spend all day at the park. Little Amy will soon get tired, but her sister will push her in a stroller. They will go on a lot of exciting rides and see some funny shows. They will also eat some different foods at the park, like cotton candy and foot-long hot dogs. *Finally,* they will go home, tired but happy. It will be a great outing.

23. A Family Outing

23. 家族旅行

The Bakers are a family of four.

貝克家共有四個成員。

John and Mary have two
children—Susan and Amy.

約翰和瑪麗有兩個小孩
——蘇珊和艾美。

Susan is eager to go to an
amusement park.

蘇珊很想要去遊樂場。

Her parents think it is not a
good idea because Amy is
too young.

她的父母認為，因為艾美
還太小，所以這不是個好
主意。

But Susan promises to help
take care of her.

但是蘇珊保證會幫忙照顧
艾美。

At last, her parents agree.

最後，她的父母同意了。

** ─────────────

outing（'autɪŋ）*n.* 郊遊；遠足
eager（'igə）*adj.* 渴望的　　***be eager to V.*** 很渴望…
amusement（ə'mjuzmənt）*n.* 娛樂
amusement park 遊樂場
promise（'prɑmɪs）*v.* 答應；保證　　***take care of*** 照顧
at last 最後　　agree（ə'gri）*v.* 同意

The family will spend all day at the park.	他們全家人將會在遊樂場裡待上一整天。
Little Amy will soon get tired, but her sister will push her in a stroller.	小艾美馬上就會感到疲倦，但是她的姊姊會用嬰兒車推著她。
They will go on a lot of exciting rides and see some funny shows.	他們會去坐很多刺激的遊樂設施，並觀賞一些有趣的表演。
They will also eat some different foods at the park, like cotton candy and foot-long hot dogs.	他們也會在遊樂場內吃一些不同的食物，像是棉花糖和特長熱狗。
Finally, they will go home, tired but happy.	最後，他們將很疲倦卻很快樂地回家。
It will be a great outing.	這將會是一次很棒的旅行。

**

spend〔spɛnd〕*v.* 度過   soon〔sun〕*adv.* 不久
tired〔taɪrd〕*adj.* 疲倦的   push〔pʊʃ〕*v.* 推
stroller〔'strolɚ〕*n.* 摺疊式嬰兒車
exciting〔ɪk'saɪtɪŋ〕*adj.* 刺激的   ride〔raɪd〕*n.* 遊樂設施
funny〔'fʌnɪ〕*adj.* 有趣的   show〔ʃo〕*n.* 表演
different〔'dɪfrənt〕*adj.* 不同的   cotton〔'kɑtn̩〕*n.* 棉花
candy〔'kændɪ〕*n.* 糖   foot〔fʊt〕*n.* 英尺
hot dog 熱狗   ***a foot-long hot dog*** 特長熱狗
finally〔'faɪnl̩ɪ〕*adv.* 最後；終於   great〔gret〕*adj.* 很棒的

TEST 24

　　請根據下方圖片的場景，描述整個事件發生的前因
後果。文章請分兩段，第一段說明之前發生了什麼
事情，並根據圖片內容描述現在的狀況；第二段請
合理說明接下來可能會發生什麼事，或者未來該做
些什麼。文長約 120 個單詞（words）左右。

The Rescue

There is a bridge over the Central River.
It is very busy at rush hour. People should
drive slowly but sometimes they do not obey
the speed limit. *One day* there was an accident.
The bridge had to be closed. Firefighters came
to rescue the drivers, who were trapped in
their cars.

The firefighters will work hard to free
the drivers. *Fortunately*, they will have only
minor injuries. They will be taken to the
hospital for treatment, and their cars will be
towed away. The bridge will reopen about
seven o'clock. *By this time*, most people will
have found another way home thanks to the
radio traffic reports. They will hope there
are no accidents on the bridge the next day.

24. The Rescue　　　　　　24. 救　援

There is a bridge over the Central River.	中央河上有一座橋。
It is very busy at rush hour.	那座橋在尖峰時間非常繁忙。
People should drive slowly but sometimes they do not obey the speed limit.	人們應該慢速行駛，但是有時候他們不遵守速限。

One day there was an accident.	有一天發生了事故。
The bridge had to be closed.	橋必須封閉。
Firefighters came to rescue the drivers, who were trapped in their cars.	消防人員前來救援被困在車內的駕駛人。

**

rescue〔ˈrɛskju〕n. v. 救援　　bridge〔brɪdʒ〕n. 橋
over〔ˈovɚ〕prep. 在⋯上面　　central〔ˈsɛntrəl〕adj. 中央的
busy〔ˈbɪzɪ〕adj. 繁忙的　　*rush hour* 尖峰時間
slowly〔ˈslolɪ〕adv. 緩慢地　　obey〔əˈbe〕v. 遵守
speed〔spid〕n. 速度　　limit〔ˈlɪmɪt〕n. 限制
speed limit 速度限制　　accident〔ˈæksədənt〕n. 事故；車禍
close〔kloz〕v. 封閉；封鎖
firefighter〔ˈfaɪrˌfaɪtɚ〕n. 消防人員
driver〔ˈdraɪvɚ〕n. 駕駛人　　trap〔træp〕v. 使困住

The firefighters will work hard to free the drivers.	消防人員將會努力地解救駕駛人。
Fortunately, they will have only minor injuries.	幸好他們只會受到輕傷。
They will be taken to the hospital for treatment, and their cars will be towed away.	他們將被送到醫院治療，而他們的車子會被拖走。
The bridge will reopen about seven o'clock.	橋大約會在七點鐘的時候重新開放。
By this time, most people will have found another way home thanks to the radio traffic reports.	在這時候，由於電台的路況報導，大部份的人將已找到替代道路回家。
They will hope there are no accidents on the bridge the next day.	他們會希望隔天這座橋上不會再有事故發生。

**

free〔fri〕*v.* 使自由；解救
fortunately〔'fɔrtʃənɪtlɪ〕*adv.* 幸運地
minor〔'maɪnə〕*adj.* 輕微的　　injury〔'ɪndʒərɪ〕*n.* 傷害
treatment〔'tritmənt〕*n.* 治療　　tow〔to〕*v.* 拖
reopen〔ri'opən〕*v.* 再開放　　*by this time* 到了這時候
way〔we〕*n.* 道路　　traffic〔'træfɪk〕*n.* 交通
report〔rɪ'port〕*n.* 報導　　*traffic report* 路況報導
the next day 隔天

TEST 25

提 示

請根據下方圖片的場景，描述整個事件發生的前因
後果。文章請分兩段，第一段說明之前發生了什麼
事情，並根據圖片內容描述現在的狀況；第二段請
合理說明接下來可能會發生什麼事，或者未來該做
些什麼。文長約 120 個單詞（words）左右。

The Camping Trip

John and Mike like to travel. Both of them are very independent, so they never go with a tour group. *Instead*, they like to travel by motorcycle. They go somewhere for the weekend on John's bike. *This weekend*, they plan to go camping in a national park. They hope the weather will be good.

Unfortunately, an unexpected weather system arrives. The temperature suddenly drops and it begins to rain. John and Mike stop at a café and wait for the rain to stop, but it continues to rain for hours. *Finally*, they decide to give up their camping trip and check into a nice hotel. The facilities there are very good and they have a lot of fun. *Despite the bad weather*, they still enjoy the weekend.

25. The Camping Trip

25. 露營之旅

John and Mike like to travel.

約翰和麥克很喜歡旅行。

Both of them are very independent, so they never go with a tour group.

他們兩人都非常獨立，所以他們從來不跟旅行團。

Instead, they like to travel by motorcycle.

取而代之的是，他們喜歡騎摩托車旅行。

They go somewhere for the weekend on John's bike.

他們週末都會騎約翰的車到某個地方。

This weekend, they plan to go camping in a national park.

這個週末，他們打算去國家公園露營。

They hope the weather will be good.

他們希望天氣會很好。

** ─────────────

camping〔'kæmpɪŋ〕*n.* 露營　　trip〔trɪp〕*n.* 旅行
travel〔'trævl〕*v.* 旅行
independent〔͵ɪndɪ'pɛndənt〕*adj.* 獨立的　　*tour group* 旅行團
instead〔ɪn'stɛd〕*adv.* 作為代替；取而代之的是
motorcycle〔'motə͵saɪkl〕*n.* 摩托車　　weekend〔'wik'ɛnd〕*n.* 週末
bike〔baɪk〕*n.* 摩托車（= *motorcycle*）
plan〔plæn〕*v.* 打算；計畫　　*national park* 國家公園
weather〔'wɛðə〕*n.* 天氣

Unfortunately, an unexpected weather system arrives.	不幸的是，出現了出乎意料的天氣。
The temperature suddenly drops and it begins to rain.	氣溫突然下降，並且開始下雨。
John and Mike stop at a café and wait for the rain to stop, but it continues to rain for hours.	約翰和麥克停在一家咖啡店等雨停，但是雨持續下了好幾個小時。
Finally, they decide to give up their camping trip and check into a nice hotel.	最後，他們決定放棄他們的露營之旅，並住在一間很棒的飯店。
The facilities there are very good and they have a lot of fun.	那裡的設備很好，他們玩得很愉快。
Despite the bad weather, they still enjoy the weekend.	儘管天氣不好，他們還是很享受這個週末假期。

✳✳ ———————————————

unfortunately〔ʌnˈfɔrtʃənɪtlɪ〕*adv.* 不幸地
unexpected〔͵ʌnɪkˈspɛktɪd〕*adj.* 出乎意料的
system〔ˈsɪstəm〕*n.* 系統   arrive〔əˈraɪv〕*v.* 到達
temperature〔ˈtɛmpərətʃə〕*n.* 氣溫
suddenly〔ˈsʌdn̩lɪ〕*adv.* 突然地   drop〔drɑp〕*v.* 下降
café〔kəˈfe〕*n.* 咖啡店   continue〔kənˈtɪnju〕*v.* 繼續
finally〔ˈfaɪn̩lɪ〕*adv.* 最後   *give up* 放棄
check into 在（旅館）辦理登記手續
facilities〔fəˈsɪlətɪz〕*n. pl.* 設施   despite〔dɪˈspaɪt〕*prep.* 儘管

TEST 26

提 示

請根據下方圖片的場景,描述整個事件發生的前因後果。文章請分兩段,第一段說明之前發生了什麼事情,並根據圖片內容描述現在的狀況;第二段請合理說明接下來可能會發生什麼事,或者未來該做些什麼。文長約 120 個單詞(words)左右。

Buying a Train Ticket

John is traveling through Europe. He travels by train because the distances are not so great. He usually buys tickets from the ticket counter. *But* he often has to wait in a long line. Someone told him that it is faster to use the automatic ticket machine. He decides to try it.

The machine will ask John to enter some information. He must indicate where he wants to go and in which class he wants to travel. *But* he does not understand the language well, so he has some trouble. *Luckily*, another traveler will help him to enter the information. *Then* John will pay by credit card. *Now that* he knows how to buy a ticket, he will do it by himself next time.

26. Buying a Train Ticket

26. 買火車票

John is traveling through
Europe.

約翰正在歐洲旅行。

He travels by train because
the distances are not so great.

因為距離不是很長,所以
他搭火車旅行。

He usually buys tickets from
the ticket counter.

他通常在售票口買票。

But he often has to wait in a
long line.

但是他時常必須排隊排很
久。

Someone told him that it is
faster to use the automatic
ticket machine.

有人告訴他,使用自動售
票機會比較快。

He decides to try it.

他決定試試看。

**

through (θru) *prep.* 遍及　　Europe ('jurəp) *n.* 歐洲
distance ('dıstəns) *n.* 距離
great (gret) *adj.* (距離、長度等) 大的
counter ('kauntɚ) *n.* 櫃台　　*ticket counter* 售票口
wait in line 排隊等候
automatic (,ɔtə'mætık) *adj.* 自動的
machine (mə'ʃin) *n.* 機器

The machine will ask John to enter some information.

售票機會要求約翰輸入一些資料。

He must indicate where he wants to go and in which class he wants to travel.

他必須指出他要去哪裡，和搭哪一種艙等旅行。

But he does not understand the language well, so he has some trouble.

但是他並不是很了解當地的語言，所以他碰到了一些困難。

Luckily, another traveler will help him to enter the information.

幸運的是，另一位旅客將會幫他輸入資料。

Then John will pay by credit card.

然後約翰會用信用卡付款。

Now that he knows how to buy a ticket, he will do it by himself next time.

既然他知道如何買票，下次他就會自己買了。

** ————————————————————

enter〔ˈɛntɚ〕v. 輸入　　information〔ˌɪnfɚˈmeʃən〕n. 資料
indicate〔ˈɪndəˌket〕v. 指出　　class〔klæs〕n. 種類；等級
language〔ˈlæŋgwɪdʒ〕n. 語言　　trouble〔ˈtrʌbḷ〕n. 困難
luckily〔ˈlʌkɪlɪ〕adv. 幸運地　　traveler〔ˈtrævlɚ〕n. 旅客
credit card 信用卡　　***now that*** 既然　　***by oneself*** 獨自

TEST 27

請根據下方圖片的場景,描述整個事件發生的前因後果。文章請分兩段,第一段說明之前發生了什麼事情,並根據圖片內容描述現在的狀況;第二段請合理說明接下來可能會發生什麼事,或者未來該做些什麼。文長約 120 個單詞(words)左右。

The Big Bike Ride

John and Pete are both keen cyclists.
They usually ride together on the weekends.
They have also entered races, though neither
of them has won one. *One day* they decided
to take a longer ride. They decided to ride
all the way across the country! *After training
hard for their journey*, they began.

John and Pete will ride their bikes for
several weeks. They will pass through all
kinds of terrain, including mountains and
plains. They will ride in all kinds of weather
—rain, cold, wind, and burning sun. It will
be a difficult journey, but it will be worth it.
They will see amazing sights and meet many
wonderful people. They will never forget
their big bike ride.

27. The Big Bike Ride　　　27. 騎腳踏車遠行

John and Pete are both keen cyclists.	約翰與彼特兩個人都是熱衷於騎腳踏車的人。
They usually ride together on the weekends.	他們通常在週末時一起騎車。
They have also entered races, though neither of them has won one.	他們也參加競賽，雖然兩人都沒得過獎。

One day they decided to take a longer ride.	有一天，他們決定要騎遠一點。
They decided to ride all the way across the country!	他們決定一路騎下去，環遊全國！
After training hard for their journey, they began.	在爲旅程努力訓練之後，他們就上路了。

** ───────────

big〔bɪg〕*adj.* 長途的　　bike〔baɪk〕*n.* 腳踏車（= *bicycle*）
ride〔raɪd〕*n.* 騎乘　　keen〔kin〕*adj.* 熱衷的；沉迷的
cyclist〔'saɪkl̩ɪst〕*n.* 騎腳踏車者　　enter〔'ɛntɚ〕*v.* 參加
race〔res〕*n.* 競賽　　neither〔'niðɚ〕*pron.* 兩者都不…
decide〔dɪ'saɪd〕*v.* 決定　　***all the way*** 一路
across〔ə'krɔs〕*prep.* 橫越　　country〔'kʌntrɪ〕*n.* 國家
train〔tren〕*v.* 受訓練　　hard〔hɑrd〕*adv.* 努力地
journey〔'dʒɝnɪ〕*n.* 旅程

John and Pete will ride their bikes for several weeks.	約翰與彼特將騎著他們的腳踏車好幾週。
They will pass through all kinds of terrain, including mountains and plains.	他們會經過各種地形,包括山區和平原。
They will ride in all kinds of weather—rain, cold, wind, and burning sun.	他們會經歷各種氣候——下雨、寒冷、刮風,和炙熱的太陽。
It will be a difficult journey, but it will be worth it.	這將是個困難的旅程,但卻是值得的。
They will see amazing sights and meet many wonderful people.	他們會看到令人驚奇的景色,並且遇到許多很棒的人。
They will never forget their big bike ride.	他們將永遠不會忘記這次的腳踏車遠行。

---

pass through 經過　　kind〔kaɪnd〕*n.* 種類
terrain〔tɛˈren〕*n.* 地形　　include〔ɪnˈklud〕*v.* 包括
mountain〔ˈmaʊntn̩〕*n.* 山　　plain〔plen〕*n.* 平原
weather〔ˈwɛðɚ〕*n.* 天氣　　wind〔wɪnd〕*n.* 風
burning〔ˈbɝnɪŋ〕*adj.* 炙熱的　　difficult〔ˈdɪfəˌkʌlt〕*adj.* 困難的
worth〔wɝθ〕*adj.* 值得的　　amazing〔əˈmezɪŋ〕*adj.* 驚人的
sight〔saɪt〕*n.* 景色　　meet〔mit〕*v.* 遇見;認識
wonderful〔ˈwʌndɚfəl〕*adj.* 很棒的

TEST 28

提 示

請根據下方圖片的場景，描述整個事件發生的前因
後果。文章請分兩段，第一段說明之前發生了什麼
事情，並根據圖片內容描述現在的狀況；第二段請
合理說明接下來可能會發生什麼事，或者未來該做
些什麼。文長約 120 個單詞（words）左右。

A Celebratory Dinner

The Wang family owns a very popular restaurant. *Every night*, the dining room is filled with customers. *On busy nights* the entire family works in the restaurant, including the children, Judy and Jimmy. Their job is to carry the delicious dishes to the tables. They like to help. They also like earning pocket money.

Judy and Jimmy are preparing dishes by adding decorations to them. *Then* they will carry them to a large table of customers. It is a family of 12 celebrating their son's graduation from university. The Wang children can see how proud the parents are of their son. They hope that they can also make their parents proud. Both of them resolve to study harder and graduate from university.

28. A Celebratory Dinner   28. 快樂的晚餐

The Wang family owns a very popular restaurant.	王家擁有一間非常受歡迎的餐廳。
Every night, the dining room is filled with customers.	每天晚上，餐廳都擠滿了顧客。
On busy nights the entire family works in the restaurant, including the children, Judy and Jimmy.	在忙碌的夜晚，全家人都會在餐廳內工作，包括他們的孩子，茱蒂和吉米。
Their job is to carry the delicious dishes to the tables.	他們的工作是把美味的菜餚端上桌。
They like to help.	他們喜歡幫忙。
They also like earning pocket money.	他們也喜歡賺零用錢。

** ——————————————

celebratory〔'sɛləbreˌtorɪ〕*adj.* 快樂的
own〔on〕*v.* 擁有　　popular〔'pɑpjələ〕*adj.* 受歡迎的
restaurant〔'rɛstərənt〕*n.* 餐廳　　***dinning room*** 餐廳
be filled with 充滿了　　customer〔'kʌstəmə〕*n.* 顧客
entire〔ɪn'taɪr〕*adj.* 整個的　　including〔ɪn'kludɪŋ〕*prep.* 包括
carry〔'kærɪ〕*v.* 端　　delicious〔dɪ'lɪʃəs〕*adj.* 美味的
dish〔dɪʃ〕*n.* 菜餚　　earn〔ɝn〕*v.* 賺
pocket〔'pɑkɪt〕*n.* 口袋　　***pocket money*** 零用錢（= *allowance*）

Judy and Jimmy are preparing
dishes by adding decorations
to them.

茱蒂和吉米在準備菜餚時
會加些裝飾。

Then they will carry them to a
large table of customers.

接著他們會將菜端到顧客
的大餐桌上。

It is a family of 12 celebrating
their son's graduation from
university.

那是個有十二個成員的家
庭，正在慶祝他們的兒子
從大學畢業。

The Wang children can see how
proud the parents are of their
son.

王家的小孩可以看出那對
父母是多麼以自己的兒子
為榮。

They hope that they can also
make their parents proud.

他們希望自己也可以讓父
母感到驕傲。

Both of them resolve to study
harder and graduate from
university.

他們兩人都決心要更努力
用功，並從大學畢業。

** ————————————

prepare〔prɪˋpɛr〕v. 準備　　add〔æd〕v. 增加
add A *to* B　把 A 加到 B 上
decoration〔͵dɛkəˋreʃən〕n. 裝飾（品）
celebrate〔ˋsɛlə͵bret〕v. 慶祝
graduation〔͵grædʒʊˋeʃən〕n. 畢業
university〔͵junəˋvɝsətɪ〕n. 大學　　proud〔praʊd〕adj. 驕傲的
be proud of　以…為榮　　resolve〔rɪˋzɑlv〕v. 決心；決定
graduate〔ˋgrædʒʊ͵et〕v. 畢業

TEST 29

請根據下方圖片的場景，描述整個事件發生的前因
後果。文章請分兩段，第一段說明之前發生了什麼
事情，並根據圖片內容描述現在的狀況；第二段請
合理說明接下來可能會發生什麼事，或者未來該做
些什麼。文長約 120 個單詞（words）左右。

The First Day of Spring

It was a beautiful spring day in the city. It seemed that the long winter was finally over at last. Many people went to the square to enjoy the warm sunshine. Some strolled around. Others simply sat on the steps and people-watched. They all hoped the good weather would continue.

Unfortunately, the warm spring weather will not last. Clouds will begin to appear in the afternoon, and soon there will be a chill in the air. Those whose took off their jackets will have to put them back on. The cold temperature will be disappointing, but not unexpected. *After all*, spring weather is changeable. Everyone will be grateful that they got to enjoy a little break from the cold winter.

29. The First Day of Spring

29. 春季的第一天

It was a beautiful spring day in the city.

這是在城市中的一個晴朗的春日。

It seemed that the long winter was finally over at last.

似乎漫長的冬天終於結束了。

Many people went to the square to enjoy the warm sunshine.

許多人到廣場去，享受溫暖的陽光。

Some strolled around.

有些人到處閒逛。

Others simply sat on the steps and people-watched.

有些就坐在階梯上看人。

They all hoped the good weather would continue.

他們都希望這樣的好天氣可以持續下去。

**　*　*** ─────────────

seem〔sim〕v. 似乎　　finally〔'faɪnḷɪ〕adv. 最後；終於
over〔'ovɚ〕adv. 結束　***at last*** 最後；終於
square〔skwɛr〕n. 廣場　　enjoy〔ɪn'dʒɔɪ〕v. 享受
warm〔wɔrm〕adj. 溫暖的　　sunshine〔'sʌn,ʃaɪn〕n. 陽光
stroll〔strol〕v. 閒逛　　around〔ə'raʊnd〕adv. 到處
simply〔'sɪmplɪ〕adv. 只　　step〔stɛp〕n. 階梯
people-watch 看人　　weather〔'wɛðɚ〕n. 天氣
continue〔kən'tɪnju〕v. 持續

Unfortunately, the warm spring weather will not last.

不幸的是，這個溫暖的春天天氣將不會持續。

Clouds will begin to appear in the afternoon, and soon there will be a chill in the air.

雲層將在下午開始出現，不久之後，空氣中就會充滿寒意。

Those whose took off their jackets will have to put them back on.

那些已脫掉外套的人，將必須再把外套穿回去。

The cold temperature will be disappointing, but not unexpected.

寒冷的天氣將會令人很失望，但卻並不令人意外。

After all, spring weather is changeable.

畢竟，春天的天氣多變化。

Everyone will be grateful that they got to enjoy a little break from the cold winter.

每個人將會很慶幸，他們能享受寒冬中的一點溫暖。

** ————————————

unfortunately〔ʌnˈfɔrtʃənɪtlɪ〕*adv.* 不幸地   last〔læst〕*v.* 持續
cloud〔klaʊd〕*n.* 雲   appear〔əˈpɪr〕*v.* 出現
soon〔sun〕*adv.* 不久   chill〔tʃɪl〕*n.* 寒意   air〔ɛr〕*n.* 空氣
take off 脫掉   jacket〔ˈdʒækɪt〕*n.* 夾客；外套
put on 穿上   temperature〔ˈtɛmpərətʃɚ〕*n.* 氣溫
disappointing〔ˌdɪsəˈpɔɪntɪŋ〕*adj.* 令人失望的
unexpected〔ˌʌnɪkˈspɛktɪd〕*adj.* 意外的   *after all* 畢竟
changeable〔ˈtʃendʒəbl̩〕*adj.* 多變的
grateful〔ˈgretfəl〕*adj.* 感激的；慶幸的   break〔brek〕*n.* 中斷

TEST 30

請根據下方圖片的場景，描述整個事件發生的前因
後果。文章請分兩段，第一段說明之前發生了什麼
事情，並根據圖片內容描述現在的狀況；第二段請
合理說明接下來可能會發生什麼事，或者未來該做
些什麼。文長約 120 個單詞（words）左右。

Overtime

This is the busy time of year at YYZ
Company. All of the employees have to work
harder than usual. The manager, Linda, also
works very hard. *Today* she had a meeting
with her staff. *After* the meeting the others
went home. *But* Linda stayed by herself in
the conference room.

She will not go home until after 10:00,
which is even later than usual. Her family
will be worried about her, but she will tell
them that she cannot help it. Her children
miss her very much. She will tell them to be
patient for a little longer. *As soon as* crisis
at work is over, she will take a vacation.
They will all go to Disney Land together.

30. Overtime 30. 加 班

This is the busy time of year at YYZ Company.

這是 XYZ 公司一年中最忙碌的時間。

All of the employees have to work harder than usual.

所有的員工都必須比平常更努力工作。

The manager, Linda, also works very hard.

經理琳達也非常努力工作。

Today she had a meeting with her staff.

今天,她和她的全體員工有個會議。

After the meeting the others went home.

在開完會之後,其他的人都回家了。

But Linda stayed by herself in the conference room.

但是琳達獨自留在會議室裡。

** ——————

overtime ('ovə‚taɪm) *n.* 加班 company ('kʌmpənɪ) *n.* 公司
employee (‚ɛmplɔɪ'i) *n.* 員工 hard (hard) *adv.* 努力地
usual ('juʒuəl) *adj.* 平常的 ***than usual*** 比平常
manager ('mænɪdʒə) *n.* 經理 meeting ('mitɪŋ) *n.* 會議
staff (stæf) *n.* 全體員工 stay (ste) *v.* 留下來
by *oneself* 獨自 conference ('kɑnfərəns) *n.* 會議
conference room 會議室

She will not go home until after 10:00, which is even later than usual.	她要一直到十點過後才會回家，那比平常還要晚很多。
Her family will be worried about her, but she will tell them that she cannot help it.	她的家人會擔心她，但是她會告訴他們她沒辦法。
Her children miss her very much.	她的孩子非常想念她。
She will tell them to be patient for a little longer.	她會告訴他們要更有耐心一點。
As soon as crisis at work is over, she will take a vacation.	當工作的關鍵時刻結束後，她會休假。
They will all go to Disney Land together.	她們會一起去迪士尼樂園。

** ——————————

family〔'fæməlɪ〕*n.* 家人　　*be worried about* 擔心
cannot help it 沒辦法　　miss〔mɪs〕*v.* 想念
patient〔'peʃənt〕*adj.* 有耐心的
for a little longer 久一點　　*as soon as* 一…就~
crisis〔'kraɪsɪs〕*n.* 危機；關鍵時刻
over〔'ovɚ〕*adv.* 結束　　*take a vacation* 休假
Disney Land 迪士尼樂園

TEST 31

提 示

請根據下方圖片的場景，描述整個事件發生的前因後果。文章請分兩段，第一段說明之前發生了什麼事情，並根據圖片內容描述現在的狀況；第二段請合理說明接下來可能會發生什麼事，或者未來該做些什麼。文長約 120 個單詞（words）左右。

A Day at the Beach

Mary and her friends went to the beach.
Mary's friends wanted to ride a banana boat.
But Mary was afraid of the water. *Finally*,
her friends persuaded her to try. They all put
on life jackets for safety. *Then* they got on
the banana boat and sped across the water.

The boat will travel at high speed back
and forth across the bay. The girls will
scream and laugh with delight, especially
Mary. *When* the boat makes a sharp turn,
all of the girls will all fall off. *However*, no
one will be hurt because they are wearing
life jackets. Mary will wonder why she was
ever afraid to try. She will want to ride the
banana boat again and again.

31. A Day at the Beach　　　31. 在海邊的一天

Mary and her friends went to the beach.	瑪麗和她的朋友到海邊。
Mary's friends wanted to ride a banana boat.	瑪麗的朋友想要坐香蕉船。
But Mary was afraid of the water.	但是瑪麗怕水。

Finally, her friends persuaded her to try.	最後，她的朋友說服了她嘗試。
They all put on life jackets for safety.	爲了安全，她們全都穿上了救生衣。
Then they got on the banana boat and sped across the water.	接著她們坐上香蕉船，並快速衝過水面。

**

beach〔bitʃ〕*n.* 海邊　　***banana boat*** 香蕉船

be afraid of 害怕　　finally〔'faɪnl̩ɪ〕*adv.* 最後；終於

persuade〔pɚ'swed〕*v.* 說服　　***put on*** 穿上

life jacket 救生衣　　safety〔'seftɪ〕*n.* 安全

get on 上（船）　　speed〔spid〕*v.* 快速前進【speed-sped-sped】

across〔ə'krɔs〕*prep.* 橫越

The boat will travel at high speed back and forth across the bay.	船將會在海灣高速地穿梭來回。
The girls will scream and laugh with delight, especially Mary.	女孩們會尖叫,並高興地大笑,尤其是瑪麗。
When the boat makes a sharp turn, all of the girls will all fall off.	當船急轉彎時,所有的女孩都會落水。
However, no one will be hurt because they are wearing life jackets.	然而,沒有人會受傷,因為她們都穿了救生衣。
Mary will wonder why she was ever afraid to try.	瑪麗會懷疑為什麼她以前會害怕嘗試。
She will want to ride the banana boat again and again.	她會想要一次又一次地搭乘香蕉船。

---

travel〔'trævḷ〕v. 前進　　speed〔spid〕n. 速度
back and forth　來回地　　bay〔be〕n. 海灣
scream〔skrim〕v. 尖叫　　delight〔dɪ'laɪt〕n. 高興
with delight　高興地　　especially〔ə'spɛʃəlɪ〕adv. 尤其是
make a turn　轉彎　　sharp〔ʃɑrp〕adj. 急轉的
fall off　落下　　hurt〔hɝt〕v. 傷害
wonder〔'wʌndɚ〕v. 懷疑;想知道　　ever〔'ɛvɚ〕adv. 曾經
again and again　一再地

TEST 32

提示

請根據下方圖片的場景，描述整個事件發生的前因後果。文章請分兩段，第一段說明之前發生了什麼事情，並根據圖片內容描述現在的狀況；第二段請合理說明接下來可能會發生什麼事，或者未來該做些什麼。文長約 120 個單詞（words）左右。

The Street Corner Band

Jack and his friends like to play music.
They often practice together at home. *But*
they are not professionals. They have never
played for an audience. *One day*, Jack wants
to play for other people to see what it is like.
They decide to play in public on a street corner.

They play on the street for a couple of
hours. *But* no matter what kind of music they
play, no one pays much attention to them.
Most people just walk by without looking at
the three musicians. *Eventually*, they feel
discouraged by the lack of interest. They
decide that it is better to play at home. All
of them are thankful that they can earn a
living at other jobs.

32. The Street Corner Band

32. 街角樂團

Jack and his friends like to
play music.

傑克和他的朋友喜歡演奏
音樂。

They often practice together
at home.

他們時常在家裡一起練習。

But they are not professionals.

但是他們不是職業的演奏者。

They have never played for
an audience.

他們從來不曾爲聽衆演奏。

One day, Jack wants to play
for other people to see what
it is like.

有一天，傑克想要爲別人
演奏，看看那是什麼樣的
情況。

They decide to play in public
on a street corner.

他們決定在一個街角公開
演奏。

** ————————————————

corner (ˈkɔrnɚ) *n.* 角落　　band (bænd) *n.* 樂團
play (ple) *v.* 演奏　　practice (ˈpræktɪs) *v.* 練習
professional (prəˈfɛʃənḷ) *n.* 以特定職業謀生的人；專業人士
audience (ˈɔdɪəns) *n.* 聽衆　　***in public*** 公開地

They play on the street for a couple of hours.

他們在街上表演了幾個小時。

But no matter what kind of music they play, no one pays much attention to them.

但無論他們演奏什麼樣的音樂，都沒有人很專心聽他們演奏。

Most people just walk by without looking at the three musicians.

大部份的人都只是從旁走過，沒有看這三位音樂家。

Eventually, they feel discouraged by the lack of interest.

最後，他們因為大家不感興趣而覺得沮喪。

They decide that it is better to play at home.

他們決定還是在家裡演奏比較好。

All of them are thankful that they can earn a living at other jobs.

他們對於自己有其他的工作可以維生心存感激。

** ——————————

a couple of 幾個　　*no matter what* 無論什麼
pay attention to 注意　　*walk by* 經過
musician〔mju'zɪʃən〕*n.* 音樂家
eventually〔ɪ'vɛntʃʊəlɪ〕*adv.* 最後
discouraged〔dɪs'kɝɪdʒd〕*adj.* 沮喪的　　lack〔læk〕*n.* 缺乏
thankful〔'θæŋkfəl〕*adj.* 感激的　　living〔'lɪvɪŋ〕*n.* 生活；生計
earn a living 謀生（ = *make a living*）

TEST 33

提 示

請根據下方圖片的場景，描述整個事件發生的前因
後果。文章請分兩段，第一段說明之前發生了什麼
事情，並根據圖片內容描述現在的狀況；第二段請
合理說明接下來可能會發生什麼事，或者未來該做
些什麼。文長約 120 個單詞（words）左右。

An Uneventful Trip

George is taking a business trip today. He will fly to Hong Kong. He arrives at the airport early. He has enough time to check in and get to his gate. The airport is big, so he takes the moving sidewalk. He is very glad that he doesn't have to run to his gate.

George's plane will leave on time and arrive in Hong Kong on time. He will meet with his clients and answer all of their questions. *After the successful meeting*, they will all have dinner together. *Then* George will return to the airport and fly home. His return flight will also be smooth. He will arrive at his house before midnight and get a good night's sleep.

33. An Uneventful Trip

33. 平淡的旅行

George is taking a business trip today.

喬治今天要出差。

He will fly to Hong Kong.

他將飛往香港。

He arrives at the airport early.

他提早到達了機場。

He has enough time to check in and get to his gate.

他有足夠的時間辦理登機手續，並到達他的登機門。

The airport is big, so he takes the moving sidewalk.

機場很大，所以他搭電動步道。

He is very glad that he doesn't have to run to his gate.

他很高興自己不必用跑的到他的登機門。

** ────────────

uneventful〔͵ʌnɪ'vɛntfəl〕*adj.* 平淡的
take a business trip 出差　　fly〔flaɪ〕*v.* 搭飛機
Hong Kong〔'haŋ'kaŋ〕*n.* 香港
airport〔'ɛr͵port〕*n.* 機場
check in 辦理登機手續　　***get to*** 到達
gate〔get〕*n.* 登機門　　take〔tek〕*v.* 搭乘
moving〔'muvɪŋ〕*adj.* 移動的
sidewalk〔'saɪd͵wɔk〕*n.* 人行道
moving sidewalk 電動步道　　glad〔glæd〕*adj.* 高興的

George's plane will leave on time and arrive in Hong Kong on time.

喬治的飛機將會準時起飛，並準時抵達香港。

He will meet with his clients and answer all of their questions.

他將和他的客戶見面，並回答他們所有的問題。

After the successful meeting, they will all have dinner together.

在成功的會議之後，他們會一起吃晚餐。

Then George will return to the airport and fly home.

接著，喬治會回到機場並搭飛機回家。

His return flight will also be smooth.

他的回程班機也將會很平順。

He will arrive at his house before midnight and get a good night's sleep.

他會在午夜之前回到家，並整夜好眠。

** ────────────────

plane〔plen〕*n.* 飛機   leave〔liv〕*v.* 出發

on time 準時   ***meet with*** 與…見面

client〔'klaɪənt〕*n.* 客戶   successful〔sək'sɛsfəl〕*adj.* 成功的

meeting〔'mitɪŋ〕*n.* 會議   have〔hæv〕*v.* 吃

return〔rɪ'tɜn〕*v.* 返回 *adj.* 回程的   flight〔flaɪt〕*n.* 班機

return flight 回程   smooth〔smuð〕*adj.* 平順的

midnight〔'mɪd,naɪt〕*n.* 午夜；半夜

a good night sleep 一夜好眠

TEST 34

提 示

請根據右方圖片的場景，描述整個事件發生的前因
後果。文章請分兩段，第一段說明之前發生了什麼
事情，並根據圖片內容描述現在的狀況；第二段請
合理說明接下來可能會發生什麼事，或者未來該做
些什麼。文長約 120 個單詞（words）左右。

A Memorable Anniversary

Barry and Cindy wanted to do something special on their wedding anniversary. They looked through the newspaper for ideas. Barry saw an advertisement for balloon rides. He thought it would be a perfect way to celebrate their special day. Cindy agreed. They drove to the field and climbed into a giant balloon.

Both of them will feel a little nervous at first. *But as* the balloon floats gently over the town, they will begin to relax. They will see their house and the church where they got married. They will open a bottle of champagne and drink a toast. *After an hour*, they will return safely to the ground. They will never forget their incredible journey or this special anniversary.

34. A Memorable Anniversary

34. 難忘的週年紀念日

Barry and Cindy wanted to do something special on their wedding anniversary.	貝瑞和辛蒂想在他們的結婚週年紀念日做一些特別的事。
They looked through the newspaper for ideas.	他們翻閱報紙尋找靈感。
Barry saw an advertisement for balloon rides.	貝瑞看到了一個搭乘熱氣球的廣告。
He thought it would be a perfect way to celebrate their special day.	他認爲這會是慶祝他們特別的日子的完美方式。
Cindy agreed.	辛蒂同意了。
They drove to the field and climbed into a giant balloon.	他們開車到那個原野，爬進了一個巨大的熱氣球。

** ————————————————

memorable〔'mɛmərəbl̩〕*adj.* 令人難忘的
anniversary〔ˌænə'vɝsərɪ〕*n.* 週年紀念日
wedding〔'wɛdɪŋ〕*n.* 婚禮　　***look through*** 翻查
advertisement〔ˌædvɚ'taɪzmənt〕*n.* 廣告
balloon〔bə'lun〕*n.* 熱氣球　　ride〔raɪd〕*n.* 搭乘
perfect〔'pɝfɪkt〕*adj.* 完美的　　way〔we〕*n.* 方式
celebrate〔'sɛləˌbret〕*v.* 慶祝　　agree〔ə'gri〕*v.* 同意
field〔fild〕*n.* 原野　　climb〔klaɪm〕*v.* 爬
giant〔'dʒaɪənt〕*adj.* 巨大的

Both of them will feel a little nervous at first.	他們兩人一開始都會覺得有點緊張。
But as the balloon floats gently over the town, they will begin to relax.	但是隨著熱氣球逐漸飄到城鎮上空，他們就會開始放鬆。
They will see their house and the church where they got married.	他們會看到他們的房子，和他們結婚時的教堂。
They will open a bottle of champagne and drink a toast.	他們會開一瓶香檳，並舉杯慶祝。
After an hour, they will return safely to the ground.	一小時之後，他們會安全地回到地面上。
They will never forget their incredible journey or this special anniversary.	他們永遠都不會忘記這個令人難以置信的旅程，或這個特別的週年紀念日。

** ————————————————

nervous〔'nɜvəs〕*adj.* 緊張的   *at first* 起初；開始
float〔flot〕*v.* 飄   gently〔'dʒɛntlɪ〕*adv.* 逐漸地
over〔'ovɚ〕*prep.* 在～上方   relax〔rɪ'læks〕*v.* 放鬆
church〔tʃɝtʃ〕*n.* 教堂   *get married* 結婚   *a bottle of* 一瓶
champagne〔ʃæm'peŋ〕*n.* 香檳   toast〔tost〕*n.* 乾杯；舉杯祝賀
drink a toast 乾杯；舉杯祝賀   return〔rɪ'tɝn〕*v.* 返回
safely〔'seflɪ〕*adv.* 安全地   ground〔graʊnd〕*n.* 地面
incredible〔ɪn'krɛdəbḷ〕*adj.* 令人難以置信的
journey〔'dʒɝnɪ〕*n.* 旅程   special〔'spɛʃəl〕*adj.* 特別的

TEST 35

提示

請根據下方圖片的場景，描述整個事件發生的前因後果。文章請分兩段，第一段說明之前發生了什麼事情，並根據圖片內容描述現在的狀況；第二段請合理說明接下來可能會發生什麼事，或者未來該做些什麼。文長約 120 個單詞（words）左右。

Local Transportation

Nicole took a trip to Europe with her family. They enjoyed going from place to place, seeing the sights. *In one city*, there were few roads. *Instead*, most of the buildings were built on canals. They wondered how to get around. *Then* they learned that most people traveled by boat!

Nicole and her family went to a "boat stop", which was much like a city bus stop. There they boarded a small open boat and began to travel down a canal. *When* they reach their destination, they will ask the boatman to stop and let them off. Nicole enjoys this means of transportation very much. She thinks it is fun to be on the water. *Best of all*, there are no traffic jams!

35. **Local Transportation**　　　35. 地方交通

Nicole took a trip to Europe with her family.	妮可和家人到歐洲旅行。
They enjoyed going from place to place, seeing the sights.	他們很喜歡四處逛、看風景。
In one city, there were few roads.	其中有個城市，道路很少。

Instead, most of the buildings were built on canals.	取而代之的是，大部份的建築物都建在運河上。
They wondered how to get around.	他們很好奇要怎麼到各個地方去。
Then they learned that most people traveled by boat!	後來他們發現大部份的人都是乘船旅行！

** ————————————

local〔'lokl̩〕*adj.* 地方的；當地的
transportation〔ˌtrænspɚ'teʃən〕*n.* 交通運輸工具
take a trip 去旅行　　Europe〔'jurəp〕*n.* 歐洲
go from place to place 到各個地方　　sight〔saɪt〕*n.* 風景
instead〔ɪn'stɛd〕*adv.* 取而代之的是；作為代替
building〔'bɪldɪŋ〕*n.* 建築物　　build〔bɪld〕*v.* 建造
canal〔kə'næl〕*n.* 運河
wonder〔'wʌndɚ〕*v.* 想知道；對…感到好奇
get around 四處走動　　travel〔'trævl̩〕*v.* 旅行；前進

Nicole and her family went to a "boat stop", which was much like a city bus stop.

妮可和她的家人走到「船站」，這就好像市區的公車站。

There they boarded a small open boat and began to travel down a canal.

他們在那裡搭上一艘開放式的小船，並開始順著運河航行。

When they reach their destination, they will ask the boatman to stop and let them off.

當他們到達目的地時，他們會要求船夫停下來，並讓他們下船。

Nicole enjoys this means of transportation very much.

妮可非常喜歡這種運輸方式。

She thinks it is fun to be on the water.

她認為在水上很有趣。

Best of all, there are no traffic jams!

最棒的是，沒有交通阻塞！

** ——————————————————

stop〔stɑp〕*n.* 站　　board〔bord〕*v.* 上（船）
open〔'opən〕*adj.* 開放式的　　down〔daʊn〕*prep.* 沿著
reach〔ritʃ〕*v.* 到達　　destination〔ˌdɛstə'neʃən〕*n.* 目的地
boatman〔'botmən〕*n.* 船夫　　means〔minz〕*n.* 方式
best of all 最棒的是　　traffic〔'træfɪk〕*n.* 交通
jam〔dʒæm〕*n.* 阻塞　　***a traffic jam*** 交通阻塞

TEST 36

提 示

請根據下方圖片的場景，描述整個事件發生的前因
後果。文章請分兩段，第一段說明之前發生了什麼
事情，並根據圖片內容描述現在的狀況；第二段請
合理說明接下來可能會發生什麼事，或者未來該做
些什麼。文長約 120 個單詞（words）左右。

Peggy's Weekend

Peggy is a very busy student. She not only goes to school, but also works. *In addition*, she is involved in many clubs. She usually goes out with her friends on weekends, but today she feels tired. She decides to stay home. She tells everyone that she has to study hard.

In fact, Peggy does not have to study at all. She just wants to relax at home alone. She will spend the weekend listening to music and reading novels. She will also write in her diary and maybe write a letter to one of her friends. *On Monday*, she will feel refreshed and ready to face the next week. *Perhaps* she will spend another relaxing weekend like this soon.

36. Peggy's Weekend

36. 佩琪的週末

Peggy is a very busy student.

佩琪是一位非常忙碌的學生。

She not only goes to school, but also works.

她不僅要上學,還要工作。

In addition, she is involved in many clubs.

此外,她還參加了很多社團。

She usually goes out with her friends on weekends, but today she feels tired.

她通常週末會和朋友出去,但是今天她覺得很累。

She decides to stay home.

她決定待在家裡。

She tells everyone that she has to study hard.

她告訴所有人,她必須用功讀書。

**

weekend ('wik'ɛnd) *n.* 週末

not only…but also~ 不僅…還~

in addition 此外　involve (ɪn'vɑlv) *v.* 使參與;使從事

be involved in 參與　club (klʌb) *n.* 社團

tired (taɪrd) *adj.* 疲倦的　decide (dɪ'saɪd) *v.* 決定

stay (ste) *v.* 停留

In fact, Peggy does not have to study at all.

事實上，佩琪根本不用念書。

She just wants to relax at home alone.

她只是想獨自在家裡放鬆。

She will spend the weekend listening to music and reading novels.

她將會花整個週末的時間聽音樂和看小說。

She will also write in her diary and maybe write a letter to one of her friends.

她也會寫日記，或許還會寫封信給她的一位朋友。

On Monday, she will feel refreshed and ready to face the next week.

到了星期一，她將會感到神清氣爽，準備好面對下一週。

Perhaps she will spend another relaxing weekend like this soon.

或許不久後，她又會渡過一個像這樣放鬆的週末。

** _____

in fact 事實上　　***not…at all*** 一點也不…　　relax〔rɪ'læks〕*v.* 放鬆
alone〔ə'lon〕*adv.* 獨自　　novel〔'nɑvl̩〕*n.* 小說
diary〔'daɪərɪ〕*n.* 日記　　refresh〔rɪ'frɛʃ〕*v.* 使提神；使神清氣爽
ready〔'rɛdɪ〕*adj.* 準備好的　　face〔fes〕*v.* 面對
perhaps〔pɚ'hæps〕*adv.* 或許
relaxing〔rɪ'læksɪŋ〕*adj.* 令人放鬆的　　soon〔sun〕*adv.* 不久

TEST 37

　　請根據下方圖片的場景，描述整個事件發生的前因
後果。文章請分兩段，第一段說明之前發生了什麼
事情，並根據圖片內容描述現在的狀況；第二段請
合理說明接下來可能會發生什麼事，或者未來該做
些什麼。文長約 120 個單詞（words）左右。

A False Alarm

It is early morning at the train station. *Several passengers* are wandering around. *Some* are going to their platform and some are meeting arriving friends. *Still others* are buying snacks or tickets. It is just like any other day at the station. *Then*, someone notices an abandoned package.

An alarm is sounded, and the police respond immediately. They tell everyone to evacuate the station and lead the passengers from the building, telling them not to panic. The bomb squad arrives soon and they investigate the suspicious package. *Fortunately*, it is not a bomb at all. Someone simply forgot her suitcase when she got on a train. The police take the suitcase to the lost and found, and the station reopens.

37. A False Alarm

37. 錯誤的警報

It is early morning at the train station.

這是一大清早的火車站。

Several passengers are wandering around.

幾位旅客正在四處閒逛。

Some are going to their platform and some are meeting arriving friends.

有些正前往他們的月台，有些是要去接即將抵達的朋友。

Still others are buying snacks or tickets.

還有一些人在買點心或車票。

It is just like any other day at the station.

車站的情況就如同往常一般。

Then, someone notices an abandoned package.

然後，有人注意到一個被遺棄的行李。

**

false〔fɔls〕*adj.* 錯誤的　　alarm〔ə'lɑrm〕*n.* 警報
train station 火車站　　passenger〔'pæsṇdʒɚ〕*n.* 旅客
wander〔'wɑndɚ〕*v.* 徘徊　　around〔ə'raʊnd〕*adv.* 到處
platform〔'plæt,fɔrm〕*n.* 月台　　meet〔mit〕*v.* 接
arrive〔ə'raɪv〕*v.* 抵達　　***still others*** 還有一些
snack〔snæk〕*n.* 點心　　ticket〔'tɪkɪt〕*n.* 車票
notice〔'notɪs〕*v.* 注意到
abandoned〔ə'bændənd〕*adj.* 被遺棄的
package〔'pækɪdʒ〕*n.* 包裹；行李

An alarm is sounded, and the police respond immediately.	警報聲響起，警察立刻做出反應。
They tell everyone to evacuate the station and lead the passengers from the building, telling them not to panic.	他們叫所有的人撤離車站，並引導乘客離開建築物，告知他們不要驚慌。
The bomb squad arrives soon and they investigate the suspicious package.	防爆小組立刻趕到，他們調查這個可疑的行李。
Fortunately, it is not a bomb at all.	幸好，它根本不是炸彈。
Someone simply forgot her suitcase when she got on a train.	只是有人上火車時忘了自己的手提箱。
The police take the suitcase to the lost and found, and the station reopens.	警察帶著那個手提箱到失物招領處，而車站就重新開放了。

**　*

sound〔saʊnd〕*v.* 使發出聲音；鳴（警報）　　***the police*** 警方
respond〔rɪ'spɑnd〕*v.* 反應　　evacuate〔ɪ'vækjʊ,et〕*v.* 撤離
lead〔lid〕*v.* 引導　　panic〔'pænɪk〕*v.* 驚慌
bomb〔bɑm〕*n.* 炸彈　　squad〔skwɑd〕*n.* 小隊
bomb squad 防爆小組　　investigate〔ɪn'vɛstə,get〕*v.* 調查
suspicious〔sə'spɪʃəs〕*adj.* 可疑的
fortunately〔'fɔrtʃənɪtlɪ〕*adv.* 幸運的是　　***not…at all*** 一點也不…
suitcase〔'sut,kes〕*n.* 手提箱　　***get on*** 搭上（交通工具）
lost and found 失物招領處　　reopen〔ri'opən〕*v.* 重新開放

TEST 38

提示

請根據下方圖片的場景，描述整個事件發生的前因後果。文章請分兩段，第一段說明之前發生了什麼事情，並根據圖片內容描述現在的狀況；第二段請合理說明接下來可能會發生什麼事，或者未來該做些什麼。文長約 120 個單詞（words）左右。

A Chance Meeting

Peggy works at a museum. She is busy preparing for a special exhibition. She will meet the artists at 2:00. *As* she enters the building, she is surprised to see her old friend Bob. Bob tells her that he is one of the artists. They both think it is a wonderful coincidence.

Peggy and Bob will attend the meeting with the other artists. *Afterward*, Peggy will invite Bob to lunch so that they can catch up. They will talk about their families and their old classmates. The exhibition will be a big success, and several of their old friends will attend. They all promise to keep in touch and have a reunion once a year. *After all*, old friends are best.

38. A Chance Meeting

38. 偶 遇

Peggy works at a museum.

佩琪在博物館工作。

She is busy preparing for a special exhibition.

她正忙於準備一個特別的展覽會。

She will meet the artists at 2:00.

她將在兩點時與藝術家們會面。

As she enters the building, she is surprised to see her old friend Bob.

當她進入大樓時,她非常驚訝地看到自己的老朋友鮑伯。

Bob tells her that he is one of the artists.

鮑伯告訴她,他是那些藝術家之一。

They both think it is a wonderful coincidence.

他們都認爲這真是太巧了。

** ───────────────

chance〔tʃæns〕*adj.* 偶然的　　meeting〔'mitɪŋ〕*n.* 會面
museum〔mju'ziəm〕*n.* 博物館　　***be busy + V-ing*** 忙於～
prepare〔prɪ'pɛr〕*v.* 準備　　special〔'spɛʃəl〕*adj.* 特別的
exhibition〔ˌɛksə'bɪʃən〕*n.* 展覽會
meet〔mit〕*v.* 和～見面　　artist〔'ɑrtɪst〕*n.* 藝術家
enter〔'ɛntɚ〕*v.* 進入　　building〔'bɪldɪŋ〕*n.* 建築物；大樓
surprised〔sə'praɪzd〕*adj.* 驚訝的
wonderful〔'wʌndəfəl〕*adj.* 很棒的
coincidence〔ko'ɪnsədəns〕*n.* 巧合

Peggy and Bob will attend the meeting with the other artists.	佩琪和鮑伯將與其他的藝術家一起參加會議。
Afterward, Peggy will invite Bob to lunch so that they can catch up.	之後，佩琪會邀請鮑伯吃午餐，這樣他們才能敘舊。
They will talk about their families and their old classmates.	他們會談論自己的家庭和他們的老同學。
The exhibition will be a big success, and several of their old friends will attend.	展覽會將會非常成功，而他們有幾個老朋友會來參加。
They all promise to keep in touch and have a reunion once a year.	他們全都承諾會保持聯絡，並每年重聚一次。
After all, old friends are best.	畢竟，老朋友是最好的。

** ————

attend〔ə'tɛnd〕 v. 參加　　afterward〔'æftəwəd〕 adv. 之後
invite〔ɪn'vaɪt〕 v. 邀請　　***catch up*** 趕上 (最新消息)
family〔'fæməlɪ〕 n. 家人　　classmate〔'klæs,met〕 n. 同學
success〔sək'sɛs〕 n. 成功　　promise〔'prɑmɪs〕 v. 承諾
keep in touch 保持聯絡　　reunion〔ri'junjən〕 n. 重聚
after all 畢竟

TEST 39

提 示

請根據下方圖片的場景，描述整個事件發生的前因
後果。文章請分兩段，第一段說明之前發生了什麼
事情，並根據圖片內容描述現在的狀況；第二段請
合理說明接下來可能會發生什麼事，或者未來該做
些什麼。文長約 120 個單詞（words）左右。

A New Hobby

Peggy went to the beach *during her vacation*. She collected many shells from the shore. She did not know what to do with them. *Then* she saw some artists painting the shells and she decided to try it. She did not think she could paint well. *However*, she was pleased with the results.

Because of this experience, Peggy will become more interested in art. She will sign up for painting class when she gets home. *Although* she is just a beginner, her teacher will think she has a lot of talent. He will urge Peggy to try new styles and to enter her work in competitions. *With this encouragement*, she will get better and better. Painting will become her favorite hobby.

39. A New Hobby　　　　39. 新的嗜好

Peggy went to the beach
during her vacation.

佩琪在放假期間前往海邊。

She collected many shells
from the shore.

她在岸邊收集了許多貝殼。

She did not know what to do
with them.

她不知道要如何處理它們。

Then she saw some artists
painting the shells and she
decided to try it.

然後她看到許多藝術家在
貝殼上作畫,她決定要試
試看。

She did not think she could
paint well.

她並不認為自己可以畫得
很好。

However, she was pleased
with the results.

然而,她對於成果感到很
滿意。

**

hobby〔'hɑbɪ〕*n.* 嗜好　　beach〔bitʃ〕*n.* 海邊
vacation〔ve'keʃən〕*n.* 假期　　collect〔kə'lɛkt〕*v.* 收集
shell〔ʃɛl〕*n.* 貝殼　　shore〔ʃor〕*n.* 海岸　　***do with*** 處理
artist〔'ɑrtɪst〕*n.* 藝術家;畫家　　paint〔pent〕*v.* 畫畫
pleased〔plizd〕*adj.* 滿意的　　result〔rɪ'zʌlt〕*n.* 成果

Because of this experience, Peggy will become more interested in art.

因為這次的經驗，佩琪會對藝術更有興趣。

She will sign up for painting class when she gets home.

當她回家時，她會報名參加繪畫課程。

Although she is just a beginner, her teacher will think she has a lot of talent.

雖然她只是個初學者，但是她的老師會覺得她很有天份。

He will urge Peggy to try new styles and to enter her work in competitions.

他會勸佩琪嘗試新的風格，並把她的作品拿去參加比賽。

With this encouragement, she will get better and better.

有了這個鼓勵，她會越來越進步。

Painting will become her favorite hobby.

繪畫會變成她最喜愛的嗜好。

** ———— ————

because of 因為　　experience〔ɪkˋspɪrɪəns〕*n.* 經驗
sign up for 報名參加　　although〔ɔlˋðo〕*conj.* 雖然
beginner〔bɪˋgɪnɚ〕*n.* 初學者　　talent〔ˋtælənt〕*n.* 天份
urge〔ɝdʒ〕*v.* 力勸；催促　　style〔staɪl〕*n.* 風格
enter〔ˋɛntɚ〕*v.* 使參加　　*enter ~ in* 使 ~ 參加（比賽）
work〔wɝk〕*n.* 作品　　competition〔͵kampəˋtɪʃən〕*n.* 比賽
encouragement〔ɪnˋkɝɪdʒmənt〕*n.* 鼓勵
favorite〔ˋfevrɪt〕*adj.* 最喜愛的

TEST 40

提示

請根據下方圖片的場景,描述整個事件發生的前因後果。文章請分兩段,第一段說明之前發生了什麼事情,並根據圖片內容描述現在的狀況;第二段請合理說明接下來可能會發生什麼事,或者未來該做些什麼。文長約 120 個單詞(words)左右。

A Good Job

Rose works in a fast-food restaurant.
She used to work in a big company, but she
was laid off. It was hard for her to find a new
job. *Finally*, she was hired to serve food.
Rose works hard to make enough money. She
is always busy in the kitchen.

Surprisingly, Rose likes her new job.
There is not too much pressure and she gets
to talk to people all day long. *Best of all*, she
never has to work overtime. *At the end of
the day*, all she has to do is clean up the
restaurant and go home. She does not make
as much money as she used to. *But* Rose
thinks that a simple life is best.

40. A Good Job

40. 一份好工作

Rose works in a fast-food restaurant.	蘿絲在一家速食餐廳工作。
She used to work in a big company, but she was laid off.	她以前在大公司裡工作，但是她被解雇了。
It was hard for her to find a new job.	對她來說，要找到一份新工作很難。
Finally, she was hired to serve food.	最後，她被雇用來供應食物。
Rose works hard to make enough money.	蘿絲努力工作以賺取足夠的錢。
She is always busy in the kitchen.	她總是在廚房裡忙碌。

** ─────────────

fast-food〔'fæst͵fud〕 *adj.* 速食的
restaurant〔'rɛstərənt〕*n.* 餐廳　　***used to V.*** 以前～
company〔'kʌmpənɪ〕*n.* 公司
lay off 解雇　　hard〔hɑrd〕*adj.* 困難的
finally〔'faɪnḷɪ〕*adv.* 最後；終於　　hire〔haɪr〕*v.* 雇用
serve〔sɝv〕*v.* 供應　　***make money*** 賺錢

Surprisingly, Rose likes her new job.	令人驚訝的是，蘿絲喜歡她的新工作。
There is not too much pressure and she gets to talk to people all day long.	這份工作沒有太多的壓力，而且她可以整天和別人說話。
Best of all, she never has to work overtime.	最棒的是，她永遠不用加班。
At the end of the day, all she has to do is clean up the restaurant and go home.	在一天結束時，她所需要做的，就是將餐廳打掃乾淨然後回家。
She does not make as much money as she used to.	她並沒有賺到像以前一樣多的錢。
But Rose thinks that a simple life is best.	但是蘿絲認為，簡單的生活是最好的。

** ────────────────

surprisingly〔səˈpraɪzɪŋlɪ〕 *adv.* 令人驚訝的是
pressure〔ˈprɛʃɚ〕 *n.* 壓力　　***get to*** 得以；能夠
all day long 整天　　***best of all*** 最棒的是
work overtime 加班
all one has to do is V. 某人所必須做的就是～
clean up 打掃　　simple〔ˈsɪmpl̩〕 *adj.* 簡單的
best〔bɛst〕 *adj.* 最好的

TEST 41

提 示

請根據下方圖片的場景,描述整個事件發生的前因
後果。文章請分兩段,第一段說明之前發生了什麼
事情,並根據圖片內容描述現在的狀況;第二段請
合理說明接下來可能會發生什麼事,或者未來該做
些什麼。文長約 120 個單詞 (words) 左右。

A New Friend

Donna lived alone. Her husband had died a few years ago and her children were grown-up. *Sometimes* she felt lonely. *Then one day* she saw a stray dog on the street. She felt sorry for the dog because it was alone, too. *So* she took it to her house.

At first the dog is afraid of Donna, but soon it learns to trust her. They go for walks together and it likes to sit with her in the living room. *Sometimes* Donna even talks to her dog! *After spending some time with her new friend* Donna will feel happier. She will also meet some new human friends when she walks the dog. They will talk about their four-legged friends.

41. A New Friend   41. 新朋友

Donna lived alone.

唐娜一個人住。

Her husband had died a few years ago and her children were grown-up.

她的丈夫幾年前過世了，而她的小孩都長大了。

Sometimes she felt lonely.

有時她會覺得寂寞。

Then one day she saw a stray dog on the street.

然後，有一天，她在街上看到一隻流浪狗。

She felt sorry for the dog because it was alone, too.

她為那隻狗感到難過，因為牠也是很孤獨的。

So she took it to her house.

所以她把那隻狗帶回家。

**

alone〔ə'lon〕*adv.* 獨自 *adj.* 孤獨的
husband〔'hʌzbənd〕*n.* 丈夫
grown-up〔'gron,ʌp〕*adj.* 成年的
lonely〔'lonlɪ〕*adj.* 寂寞的
stray〔stre〕*adj.* 走失的   *stray dog* 流浪狗
sorry〔'sɔrɪ〕*adj.* 遺憾的；難過的

At first the dog is afraid of Donna, but soon it learns to trust her.

起初這隻狗很怕唐娜，但是牠很快就學會信任她。

They go for walks together and it likes to sit with her in the living room.

他們一起散步，而且牠喜歡在客廳裡坐在她旁邊。

Sometimes Donna even talks to her dog!

有時候唐娜甚至會跟狗說話！

After spending some time with her new friend Donna will feel happier.

在花了許多時間與她的新朋友相處後，唐娜將會感到更快樂。

She will also meet some new human friends when she walks the dog.

當她遛狗時，她也會結交一些新的人類朋友。

They will talk about their four-legged friends.

他們會一起討論他們四隻腳的朋友。

**

at first 起初；一開始　　*be afraid of* 害怕

trust〔trʌst〕*v.* 信任　　*go for a walk* 去散步

meet〔mit〕*v.* 認識　　human〔ˈhjumən〕*adj.* 人類的

walk〔wɔk〕*v.* 遛（狗）　　*four-legged* *adj.* 四隻腳的

TEST 42

提 示

請根據下方圖片的場景，描述整個事件發生的前因
後果。文章請分兩段，第一段說明之前發生了什麼
事情，並根據圖片內容描述現在的狀況；第二段請
合理說明接下來可能會發生什麼事，或者未來該做
些什麼。文長約 120 個單詞（words）左右。

A New Experience

Wendy took a trip to Thailand. She was
nervous about traveling to a foreign country.
She knew that some things there would be
very different. She went to see an elephant
show. The elephant trainer asked for a
volunteer. *Before she knew it*, Wendy's
friends had pushed her into the ring!

The trainer brings her over to two
elephants and asks her to sit on their trunks.
At first, Wendy is terrified, but the elephants
are gentle and she begins to relax. She is
amazed by the size and strength of the
animals. Her friends take a lot of pictures of
her. *When* she goes home, she will show the
photos to her family. Everyone will
congratulate her for being so brave.

42. A New Experience　　42. 新的體驗

Wendy took a trip to Thailand.

溫蒂到泰國去旅行。

She was nervous about traveling to a foreign country.

對於到國外旅行，她感到很緊張。

She knew that some things there would be very different.

她知道那裡的某些事物會很不一樣。

She went to see an elephant show.

她去看了一場大象表演。

The elephant trainer asked for a volunteer.

大象訓練師要找一位自願者。

Before she knew it, Wendy's friends had pushed her into the ring!

在溫蒂意識到之前，她的朋友就已經將她推到圓形表演場中了！

＊＊ ─────────────

experience〔ɪk'spɪrɪəns〕*n.* 體驗　　***take a trip*** 去旅行
Thailand〔'taɪlənd〕*n.* 泰國　　nervous〔'nɝvəs〕*adj.* 緊張的
travel〔'trævl̩〕*v.* 旅行　　foreign〔'fɔrɪn〕*adj.* 外國的
country〔'kʌntrɪ〕*n.* 國家　　show〔ʃo〕*n.* 表演
trainer〔'trenɚ〕*n.* 馴獸師　　***ask for*** 要求
volunteer〔͵vɑlən'tɪr〕*n.* 自願者
before sb. knew it 在某人意識到之前　　push〔puʃ〕*v.* 推
ring〔rɪŋ〕*n.* 圓形表演場

The trainer brings her over to two elephants and asks her to sit on their trunks.

馴獸師把她帶到兩隻大象那裡，並要求她坐在大象的鼻子上。

At first, Wendy is terrified, but the elephants are gentle and she begins to relax.

起初，溫蒂很害怕，但是大象們很溫柔，所以她就開始放輕鬆。

She is amazed by the size and strength of the animals.

她對大象的體型和力氣感到很驚訝。

Her friends take a lot of pictures of her.

她的朋友幫她拍了很多照片。

When she goes home, she will show the photos to her family.

當她回家時，她會把照片拿給家人看。

Everyone will congratulate her for being so brave.

每個人都會恭喜她這麼勇敢。

** ────────────────────

bring sb. over to 把某人帶往   trunk〔trʌŋk〕*n.* 象鼻

at first 起初；一開始   terrified〔'tɛrə,faɪd〕*adj.* 害怕的

gentle〔'dʒɛntḷ〕*adj.* 溫柔的   relax〔rɪ'læks〕*v.* 放輕鬆

amaze〔ə'mez〕*v.* 使驚訝   size〔saɪz〕*n.* 大小；尺寸

strength〔strɛŋθ〕*n.* 力量   ***take pictures*** 拍照

show〔ʃo〕*v.* 把…給~看   photo〔'foto〕*n.* 照片

family〔'fæməlɪ〕*n.* 家人

congratulate〔kən'grætʃə,let〕*v.* 恭喜

brave〔brev〕*adj.* 勇敢的

TEST 43

提示

請根據下方圖片的場景，描述整個事件發生的前因後果。文章請分兩段，第一段說明之前發生了什麼事情，並根據圖片內容描述現在的狀況；第二段請合理說明接下來可能會發生什麼事，或者未來該做些什麼。文長約 120 個單詞（words）左右。

The Scary Bridge

There is a popular temple in the mountains. Many tourists like to visit it. *However*, there are no roads there, so they must walk through the forest. Halfway to the temple there is a gorge. The only way across is a long, narrow bridge. Many people are afraid of the bridge.

The guide will give the tourists some advice for crossing the bridge. He will tell them to walk slowly and gently. *Most important of all*, they must not look down! Some people will say they cannot do it; they will want to turn back. *But* their friends will encourage them, and everyone will cross the bridge. They will enjoy their time at the temple, but then they will have to face the scary bridge again!

43. **The Scary Bridge**　　　　43. 可怕的橋

There is a popular temple in the mountains.

在山裡面有一間很受歡迎的廟。

Many tourists like to visit it.

許多遊客都喜歡去那裡。

However, there are no roads there, so they must walk through the forest.

然而，那裡沒有路，所以他們必須走過森林。

Halfway to the temple there is a gorge.

在前往廟的途中，有一個峽谷。

The only way across is a long, narrow bridge.

唯一能橫越到對面的路，是一座狹長的橋。

Many people are afraid of the bridge.

許多人都很害怕這座橋。

**——————————————

scary (ˈskɛrɪ) adj. 可怕的　　bridge (brɪdʒ) n. 橋
popular (ˈpɑpjələ) adj. 受歡迎的　　temple (ˈtɛmpl̩) n. 廟
in the mountain 在山區　　tourist (ˈturɪst) n. 遊客
visit (ˈvɪzɪt) v. 參觀；拜訪；去　　*walk through* 走過；經過
forest (ˈfɔrɪst) n. 森林　　halfway (ˈhæfˈwe) adv. 在中途
gorge (gɔrdʒ) n. 峽谷　　way (we) n. 路
across (əˈkrɔs) adv. 橫越（到對面）
narrow (ˈnæro) adj. 狹窄的　　*be afraid of* 害怕

The guide will give the tourists some advice for crossing the bridge.

導遊會給遊客一些過橋的建議。

He will tell them to walk slowly and gently.

他會告訴他們要緩慢而且輕輕地過橋。

Most important of all, they must not look down!

最重要的是，他們絕對不能往下看！

Some people will say they cannot do it; they will want to turn back.

有些人會說他們辦不到；他們會想要回頭。

But their friends will encourage them, and everyone will cross the bridge.

但是他們的朋友會鼓勵他們，所有人都會過橋。

They will enjoy their time at the temple, but then they will have to face the scary bridge again!

他們在那間廟裡會玩得很愉快，但是接著他們又必須再次面對那座可怕的橋！

** —————————————————

guide〔gaɪd〕*n.* 導遊   advice〔əd'vaɪs〕*n.* 建議
cross〔krɔs〕*v.* 越過   slowly〔'slolɪ〕*adv.* 緩慢地
gently〔'dʒɛntlɪ〕*adv.* 輕輕地   ***most important of all*** 最重要的是
must + not + V. 絕不能～   ***look down*** 往下看
turn back 返回   encourage〔ɪn'kɝɪdʒ〕*v.* 鼓勵
face〔fes〕*v.* 面對

TEST 44

提示

請根據下方圖片的場景，描述整個事件發生的前因
後果。文章請分兩段，第一段說明之前發生了什麼
事情，並根據圖片內容描述現在的狀況；第二段請
合理說明接下來可能會發生什麼事，或者未來該做
些什麼。文長約 120 個單詞（words）左右。

The Train to School

Annie lives in a suburb, and her school is in the city. *Every day* she takes a commuter train to school. *One day* she woke up too late and she missed the train. She did not know how to get to her school. *Then* she had a good idea. She would follow the railway tracks!

Annie will walk along the tracks until she gets to the next station, where her school is. *Fortunately*, she will not meet a train along the way! The stationmaster will be very surprised to see her. He will be shocked that she walked along the tracks because it is dangerous. Annie will promise not to do it again. *Then* she will go to her school on time.

44. The Train to School

44. 去學校的火車

Annie lives in a suburb, and her school is in the city.

安妮住在郊區,而她的學校在市區。

Every day she takes a commuter train to school.

她每天都搭通勤火車到學校。

One day she woke up too late and she missed the train.

有一天,她太晚起床,錯過了火車。

She did not know how to get to her school.

她不知道要如何去學校。

Then she had a good idea.

然後,她有了一個好主意。

She would follow the railway tracks!

她要沿著鐵軌前進!

**

suburb〔'sʌbɝb〕*n.* 郊區   take〔tek〕*v.* 搭乘
commuter〔kə'mjutɚ〕*n.* 通勤者
commuter train 通勤火車   ***wake up*** 起床
late〔let〕*adv.* 晚   miss〔mɪs〕*v.* 錯過
get to 到達   follow〔'falo〕*v.* 順著(道路)前進
railway〔'rel,we〕*n.* 鐵路   track〔træk〕*n.* 軌道

Annie will walk along the tracks until she gets to the next station, where her school is.	安妮會沿著軌道走,直到她到達下一站,也就是學校的所在地。
Fortunately, she will not meet a train along the way!	幸運的是,她一路上都不會遇到火車!
The stationmaster will be very surprised to see her.	火車站站長看到她將會非常驚訝。
He will be shocked that she walked along the tracks because it is dangerous.	他會很震驚,是因為她沿著軌道走很危險。
Annie will promise not to do it again.	安妮會保證不會再這麼做了。
Then she will go to her school on time.	然後她會準時到達學校。

**

along〔ə'lɔŋ〕*prep.* 沿著
fortunately〔'fɔrtʃənɪtlɪ〕*adv.* 幸運地
meet〔mit〕*v.* 遇見   *along the way* 一路上
stationmaster〔'steʃən,mæstɚ〕*n.* 火車站站長
surprised〔sə'praɪzd〕*adj.* 驚訝的
shocked〔ʃɑkt〕*adj.* 震驚的
promise〔'prɑmɪs〕*v.* 保證   *on time* 準時

TEST 45

　　請根據下方圖片的場景，描述整個事件發生的前因
後果。文章請分兩段，第一段說明之前發生了什麼
事情，並根據圖片內容描述現在的狀況；第二段請
合理說明接下來可能會發生什麼事，或者未來該做
些什麼。文長約 120 個單詞（words）左右。

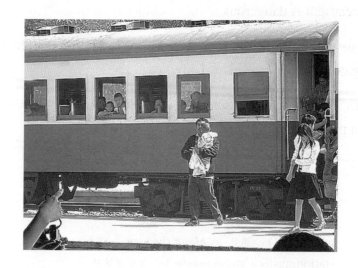

A Long Journey

A train was traveling through the countryside.
It was full of people going home for a holiday.
Normally, the journey takes four hours.
However, there was a problem. The track ahead
was damaged and the train could not proceed.
It pulled into a station and stopped.

The people on the train will have to wait a
long time because the track cannot be repaired
quickly. *Unfortunately*, it is not easy to continue
by bus from this small town. *Therefore*, the
passengers will stay on the train or in the station.
Some vendors will appear to sell them food and
water. *Finally*, the track will reopen and their
journey will continue. *Altogether* it will take
them sixteen hours to get home.

45. **A Long Journey**

45. 漫長的旅程

A train was traveling through
the countryside.

一輛火車正行駛於鄉間。

It was full of people going home
for a holiday.

它載滿了要回家過節的人。

Normally, the journey takes four
hours.

一般說來，車程是四小時。

However, there was a problem.

然而，有問題發生了。

The track ahead was damaged
and the train could not proceed.

前方的鐵軌受損，火車無法
前進。

It pulled into a station and
stopped.

火車開進某個車站並且停
了下來。

**

journey〔'dʒɜnɪ〕*n.* 旅程　　travel〔'trævl̩〕*v.* 旅行；行進
through〔θru〕*prep.* 穿越
countryside〔'kʌntrɪ͵saɪd〕*n.* 鄉間
be full of 充滿了　　holiday〔'hɑlə͵de〕*n.* 假日
normally〔'nɔrml̩ɪ〕*adv.* 通常　　take〔tek〕*v.* 花費
track〔træk〕*n.* 軌道　　ahead〔ə'hɛd〕*adv.* 在前方
damage〔'dæmɪdʒ〕*v.* 損害　　proceed〔prə'sid〕*v.* 前進
pull into 停靠；停進…

The people on the train will have to wait a long time because the track cannot be repaired quickly.

火車上的人將必須等很久，因為鐵軌無法很快地修好。

Unfortunately, it is not easy to continue by bus from this small town.

不幸的是，要從這個小鎮坐公車繼續前進並不容易。

Therefore, the passengers will stay on the train or in the station.

因此，乘客將會留在火車上或車站內。

Some vendors will appear to sell them food and water.

有些小販會出現，販賣食物和水。

Finally, the track will reopen and their journey will continue.

最後，軌道會重新開放，而他們的旅程將會繼續。

Altogether it will take them sixteen hours to get home.

他們總共花了十六個小時才到家。

**

repair〔rɪ'pɛr〕v. 修理

unfortunately〔ʌn'fɔrtʃənɪtlɪ〕adv. 不幸地

continue〔kən'tɪnju〕v. 繼續

passenger〔'pæsn̩dʒɚ〕n. 乘客

vendor〔'vɛndɚ〕n. 小販　　appear〔ə'pɪr〕v. 出現

finally〔'faɪnl̩ɪ〕adv. 最後　　reopen〔ri'opən〕v. 重新開放

altogether〔͵ɔltə'gɛðɚ〕adv. 總共

TEST 46

提 示

請根據下方圖片的場景，描述整個事件發生的前因後果。文章請分兩段，第一段說明之前發生了什麼事情，並根據圖片內容描述現在的狀況；第二段請合理說明接下來可能會發生什麼事，或者未來該做些什麼。文長約 120 個單詞（words）左右。

The Garage Sale

Mrs. Johnson lives in a big house. She has collected a lot of things over the years. *Now* she wants to get rid of some of them. She has decided to have a garage sale. She displays the things she no longer wants on long tables. People come to have a look.

One woman wants to buy a picture. *However*, she thinks the price is too high because it is used. Mrs. Johnson agrees that the picture is old, but she says that only makes it more valuable. Mrs. Johnson and the woman bargain and then finally agree on a price. The woman writes a check for $20. *At the end of the day*, Mrs. Johnson will have sold most of her old things.

46. The Garage Sale

46. 舊貨出售

Mrs. Johnson lives in a big house.

強森太太住在一棟大房子裡。

She has collected a lot of things over the years.

多年來她收集了很多東西。

Now she wants to get rid of some of them.

現在，她想要賣掉一些。

She has decided to have a garage sale.

她決定要辦個舊貨出售。

She displays the things she no longer wants on long tables.

她在長桌上展示她不再想要的東西。

People come to have a look.

人們都過來看一看。

**

garage〔gə'rɑʒ〕*n.* 車庫　　sale〔sel〕*n.* 出售
garage sale （在車庫中進行之）舊貨出售
collect〔kə'lɛkt〕*v.* 收集
over〔'ovɚ〕*prep.* 在…期間
get rid of 擺脫；賣掉　　display〔dɪ'sple〕*v.* 展示
no longer 不再　　***have a look*** 看一看

One woman wants to buy a picture.

有位婦人想買一幅畫。

However, she thinks the price is too high because it is used.

然而，她覺得價格太高，因爲畫很老舊。

Mrs. Johnson agrees that the picture is old, but she says that only makes it more valuable.

強森太太同意那幅畫很舊，但是她說這只會讓它更有價值。

Mrs. Johnson and the woman bargain and then finally agree on a price.

強森太太和那位婦人討價還價，最後終於在價錢上取得共識。

The woman writes a check for $20.

那位婦人寫了一張二十元美金的支票。

At the end of the day, Mrs. Johnson will have sold most of her old things.

到那天結束時，強森太太將會賣掉她大部份的舊東西。

** ——————————

used〔juzd〕*adj.* 老舊的　　agree〔ə'gri〕*v.* 同意
valuable〔'væljəbḷ〕*adj.* 有價值的
bargain〔'bɑrgɪn〕*v.* 討價還價
finally〔'faɪnḷɪ〕*adv.* 最後；終於
agree on 同意；對…取得一致意見　　check〔tʃɛk〕*n.* 支票

TEST 47

提示

請根據下方圖片的場景，描述整個事件發生的前因
後果。文章請分兩段，第一段說明之前發生了什麼
事情，並根據圖片內容描述現在的狀況；第二段請
合理說明接下來可能會發生什麼事，或者未來該做
些什麼。文長約 120 個單詞（words）左右。

Alligator Alley

When Mr. Brown was a young boy, he
liked animals very much. He especially liked
reptiles. He really wanted to have one as a
pet. *However*, his parents would not allow
it. *When* he grew up, Mr. Brown bought an
alligator. This alligator had babies, and soon
Mr. Brown had hundreds of alligators.

It is expensive to feed so many alligators,
so he decides to open a tourist attraction. He
calls it Alligator Alley. Visitors can look at
the big animals for a small fee. They
especially like to come at feeding time when
the alligators open their mouths wide. Mr.
Brown will teach people a lot about reptiles.
Then people will fear the creatures less and
like them more.

47. Alligator Alley

47. 鱷魚街

When Mr. Brown was a young boy, he liked animals very much.

當伯朗先生還是小男孩的時候,他非常喜歡動物。

He especially liked reptiles.

他尤其喜歡爬蟲類。

He really wanted to have one as a pet.

他真的很想養一隻當寵物。

However, his parents would not allow it.

然而,他的父母並不允許。

When he grew up, Mr. Brown bought an alligator.

當伯朗先生長大後,他買了一隻鱷魚。

This alligator had babies, and soon Mr. Brown had hundreds of alligators.

這隻鱷魚生了小孩,很快地,伯朗先生就了有好幾百隻鱷魚。

**

---

alligator〔'ælə,getə〕n. 短吻鱷　　alley〔'ælɪ〕n. 巷子
especially〔ə'spɛʃəlɪ〕adv. 尤其;特別是
reptile〔'rɛptl̩〕n. 爬蟲類　　pet〔pɛt〕n. 寵物
allow〔ə'laʊ〕v. 允許　　***grow up*** 長大
baby〔'bebɪ〕n. 幼獸　　***hundreds of*** 數以百計的

It is expensive to feed so many alligators, so he decides to open a tourist attraction.

要餵這麼多鱷魚是很貴的，所以他決定開設一個觀光景點。

He calls it Alligator Alley.

他稱它爲鱷魚街。

Visitors can look at the big animals for a small fee.

觀光客可以付一點入場費看這些大型動物。

They especially like to come at feeding time when the alligators open their mouths wide.

他們特別喜歡在餵食時間來看，那時鱷魚會大大地張開嘴巴。

Mr. Brown will teach people a lot about reptiles.

伯朗先生會教導人們許多有關爬蟲類的知識。

Then people will fear the creatures less and like them more.

然後人們就會比較不怕這種動物，而會比較喜歡牠們。

**

feed〔fid〕v. 餵　　tourist〔'turɪst〕adj. 觀光的
attraction〔ə'trækʃən〕n. 景點　　call〔kɔl〕v. 稱…
visitor〔'vɪzɪtɚ〕n. 觀光客　　fee〔fi〕n. 費用
feeding time 餵食時間　　mouth〔mauθ〕n. 嘴巴
wide〔waɪd〕adv. 張大地　　fear〔fɪr〕v. 害怕
creature〔'kritʃɚ〕n. 生物；動物

TEST 48

提 示

請根據下方圖片的場景，描述整個事件發生的前因後果。文章請分兩段，第一段說明之前發生了什麼事情，並根據圖片內容描述現在的狀況；第二段請合理說明接下來可能會發生什麼事，或者未來該做些什麼。文長約 120 個單詞（words）左右。

Pretzel Surprise

Mrs. Smith and her children were shopping at the mall. *After a while*, they began to feel hungry. They looked for someplace to eat, but there were long lines everywhere. *Then* the children saw a pretzel stand. There was no line. They asked their mother if they could try it.

Mrs. Smith thinks that pretzels are not very tasty and that they cannot be a meal. *But when* she gets to the counter, she is surprised. The pretzels are very big! They also come in many varieties, and they smell delicious. They each order a different kind of pretzel so that they can taste three kinds. Mrs. Smith likes them so much that she orders some more to take home for Mr. Smith.

48. Pretzel Surprise   48. 捲餅驚喜

Mrs. Smith and her children were shopping at the mall.

史密斯太太和她的小孩在購物中心裡購物。

After a while, they began to feel hungry.

不久之後,他們開始覺得很餓。

They looked for someplace to eat, but there were long lines everywhere.

他們想找地方吃東西,但是到處都大排長龍。

Then the children saw a pretzel stand.

然後,孩子們看到一個捲餅攤。

There was no line.

那裡沒有人排隊。

They asked their mother if they could try it.

他們問他們的媽媽能不能試試看。

** ———————————————

pretzel (ˈprɛtsḷ) *n.* 鹹脆捲餅   surprise (səˈpraɪz) *n.* 驚喜
shop (ʃɑp) *v.* 購物   mall (mɔl) *n.* 購物中心
hungry (ˈhʌŋgrɪ) *adj.* 飢餓的   ***look for*** 尋找
someplace (ˈsʌmˌples) *adv.* 某處
stand (stænd) *n.* 攤位   line (laɪn) *n.* 行列
everywhere (ˈɛvrɪˌhwɛr) *adv.* 到處   if (ɪf) *conj.* 是否

Mrs. Smith thinks that pretzels are not very tasty and that they cannot be a meal.

史密斯太太認爲捲餅不太好吃，而且不能當正餐。

But when she gets to the counter, she is surprised.

但是當她走到櫃台時，她非常驚訝。

The pretzels are very big!

捲餅相當大！

They also come in many varieties, and they smell delicious.

它們也有很多種類，而且聞起來很美味。

They each order a different kind of pretzel so that they can taste three kinds.

他們每個人都點了不同種類的捲餅，這樣他們就可以嚐三種口味。

Mrs. Smith likes them so much that she orders some more to take home for Mr. Smith.

史密斯太太非常喜歡，所以她又點了一些帶回家給史密斯先生。

** ─────────────

tasty（'testɪ）*adj.* 好吃的　　meal（mil）*n.* 一餐　　***get to*** 到達
counter（'kaʊntɚ）*n.* 櫃台　　surprised（sə'praɪzd）*adj.* 驚訝的
come in 有（…種類、形狀、尺寸、顏色等）
variety（və'raɪətɪ）*n.* 種類；變化　　smell（smɛl）*v.* 聞起來
delicious（dɪ'lɪʃəs）*adj.* 美味的　　order（'ɔrdɚ）*v.* 點（菜）
kind（kaɪnd）*n.* 種類　　***so that*** 以便於
taste（test）*v.* 品嚐　　***so…that~*** 如此…以致於~

TEST 49

提 示

請根據下方圖片的場景，描述整個事件發生的前因
後果。文章請分兩段，第一段說明之前發生了什麼
事情，並根據圖片內容描述現在的狀況；第二段請
合理說明接下來可能會發生什麼事，或者未來該做
些什麼。文長約 120 個單詞（words）左右。

Parasailing

Mary's friends wanted to go to the beach. *But* she does not like the beach because she thinks that it is boring to sit on the sand. *However*, she agrees to go. *At the beach*, Mary sees some people floating in the air. They are parasailing! She decides to try it.

Mary pays for the trip and receives some instruction. *Then* she puts on a life jacket and a helmet. *Finally*, she is strapped into the parachute, which is attached to a boat. The boat speeds across the water and Mary rises into the air! *Soon* she is floating high above the water, but she does not feel scared at all. It is a trip to the beach that she will never forget.

49. **Parasailing**

49. 拖曳傘

Mary's friends wanted to go to the beach.

瑪麗的朋友想要去海邊。

But she does not like the beach because she thinks that it is boring to sit on the sand.

但是她不喜歡海邊，因為她認為坐在沙灘上很無聊。

However, she agrees to go.

然而，她同意前往。

At the beach, Mary sees some people floating in the air.

在海邊，瑪麗看到有些人飄浮在空中。

They are parasailing!

他們在玩拖曳傘！

She decides to try it.

她決定要試試看。

** ─────────────

parasailing〔'pærə,selɪŋ〕*n.* 拖曳傘；帆傘運動　*v.* 玩拖曳傘
beach〔bitʃ〕*n.* 海邊　　boring〔'borɪŋ〕*adj.* 無聊的
sand〔sænd〕*n.* 沙子；沙灘　　agree〔ə'gri〕*v.* 同意
float〔flot〕*v.* 飄浮　　***in the air*** 在空中

Mary pays for the trip and receives some instruction.	瑪麗付了錢，並接受一些指導。
Then she puts on a life jacket and a helmet.	接著，她穿上救生衣並戴上安全帽。
Finally, she is strapped into the parachute, which is attached to a boat.	最後，她被綁在裝附在船上的降落傘上。
The boat speeds across the water and Mary rises into the air!	船快速行駛過水面，而瑪麗就升到空中！
Soon she is floating high above the water, but she does not feel scared at all.	很快的，她高高地飄浮在水上，但是她一點都不覺得害怕。
It is a trip to the beach that she will never forget.	這是一趟她將永遠不會忘記的海灘之旅。

** ────────────────

pay for 付…錢　　trip〔trɪp〕*n.* 旅程
receive〔rɪˈsiv〕*v.* 收到　　instruction〔ɪnˈstrʌkʃən〕*n.* 指導
put on 穿上　　*life jacket* 救生衣
helmet〔ˈhɛlmɪt〕*n.* 安全帽；頭盔　　finally〔ˈfaɪnl̩ɪ〕*adv.* 最後
strap〔stræp〕*v.* 用皮條綑綁　　parachute〔ˈpærəˌʃut〕*n.* 降落傘
attach〔əˈtætʃ〕*v.* 使裝上；使附上　　*be attached to* 附置在…
speed〔spid〕*v.* 快速前進　　across〔əˈkrɔs〕*prep.* 橫越
rise〔raɪz〕*v.* 上升　　high〔haɪ〕*adv.* 高高地
above〔əˈbʌv〕*prep.* 在…之上　　scared〔skɛrd〕*adj.* 害怕的
not…at all 一點也不…

TEST 50

提 示

請根據下方圖片的場景，描述整個事件發生的前因
後果。文章請分兩段，第一段說明之前發生了什麼
事情，並根據圖片內容描述現在的狀況；第二段請
合理說明接下來可能會發生什麼事，或者未來該做
些什麼。文長約 120 個單詞（words）左右。

The Wonderful Internet

Bob is a manager. He often attends meetings, but he thinks that they waste a lot of time. He prefers to communicate with people by using the Internet. *So* he often sends email to his colleagues. One of his colleagues cannot understand the document he sent. He wants to have a meeting with Bob.

Instead of having a meeting, Bob will use the Internet. He will use a voice program to talk with his colleague. Both of them are using their computer, so they can see the same document. Bob will explain what he wants to his colleague and solve the problem. He will do it all without leaving his office. He will be very glad to have avoided another meeting!

50. **The Wonderful Internet**

50. 很棒的網路

Bob is a manager.	鮑伯是個經理。
He often attends meetings, but he thinks that they waste a lot of time.	他時常參加會議,但是他認為那樣浪費很多時間。
He prefers to communicate with people by using the Internet.	他比較喜歡用網路與人溝通。

So he often sends email to his colleagues.	所以他時常寄電子郵件給他的同事。
One of his colleagues cannot understand the document he sent.	其中一位同事不了解他寄的文件。
He wants to have a meeting with Bob.	他想要與鮑伯開個會。

** ———————————————

wonderful〔'wʌndəfəl〕*adj.* 很棒的
Internet〔'ıntɚ‚nɛt〕*n.* 網際網路　　manager〔'mænıdʒɚ〕*n.* 經理
attend〔ə'tɛnd〕*v.* 參加　　meeting〔'mitıŋ〕*n.* 會議
prefer〔prı'fɝ〕*v.* 比較喜歡
communicate〔kə'mjunə‚ket〕*v.* 溝通
send〔sɛnd〕*v.* 寄　　email〔'i‚mel〕*n.* 電子郵件 (= *e-mail*)
colleague〔'kɑlig〕*n.* 同事 (= *co-worker*)
document〔'dɑkjəmənt〕*n.* 文件

Instead of having a meeting, Bob will use the Internet.

鮑伯將會使用網路，而不是開會。

He will use a voice program to talk with his colleague.

他會使用語音軟體來和他的同事交談。

Both of them are using their computer, so they can see the same document.

他們兩人都使用自己的電腦，所以他們可以看相同的文件。

Bob will explain what he wants to his colleague and solve the problem.

鮑伯會向他的同事解釋他要什麼，並解決問題。

He will do it all without leaving his office.

他不用離開辦公室，就能把所有的事情完成。

He will be very glad to have avoided another meeting!

他會非常高興避開了另一次會議！

**

instead of 而不是　　voice〔vɔɪs〕*n.* 聲音
program〔'progræm〕*n.* 軟體　　*the same* 相同的
explain〔ɪk'splen〕*v.* 解釋；說明　　solve〔sɑlv〕*v.* 解決
problem〔'prɑbləm〕*n.* 問題　　office〔'ɔfɪs〕*n.* 辦公室
glad〔glæd〕*adj.* 高興的　　avoid〔ə'vɔɪd〕*v.* 避開

如何寫看圖英作文 ②

主　　　編 / 劉　毅

發　行　所 / 學習出版有限公司　　☎ (02) 2704-5525

郵 撥 帳 號 / 0512727-2 學習出版社帳戶

登　記　證 / 局版台業 2179 號

印　刷　所 / 裕強彩色印刷有限公司

台 北 門 市 / 台北市許昌街 10 號 2 F　　☎ (02) 2331-4060

台灣總經銷 / 紅螞蟻圖書有限公司　　☎ (02) 2795-3656

美國總經銷 / Evergreen Book Store　　☎ (818) 2813622

本公司網址　www.learnbook.com.tw

電 子 郵 件　learnbook@learnbook.com.tw

售價：新台幣一百八十元正

2013 年 5 月 1 日二版二刷

ISBN 978-986-231-104-2